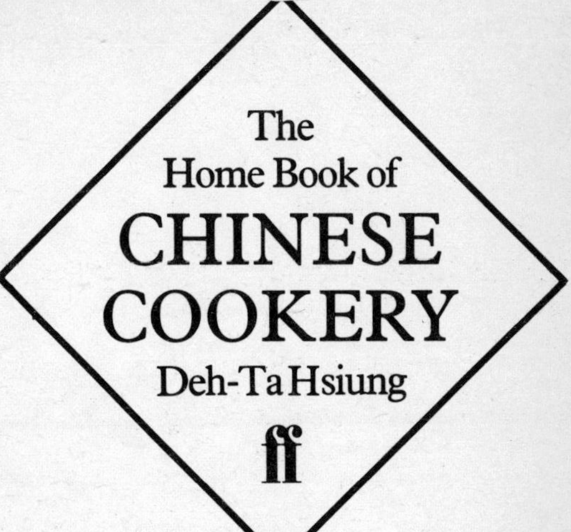

faber and faber
LONDON · BOSTON

First published in 1978 by
Faber and Faber Limited
3 Queen Square London WC1N 3AU
This revised edition published in 1987

Photoset by Parker Typesetting Service Leicester
Printed in Great Britain by
Richard Clay Ltd Bungay Suffolk

British Library Cataloguing in Publication Data

Hsiung, Deh-Ta
The Home Book of Chinese Cookery — 2nd ed.
1. Cookery, Chinese
I. Title II. Hsiung, Deh-Ta.
641.5951 TX724.5.C5

ISBN 0-571-13884-5

This book is dedicated to
my mother Dymia Tsai Hsiung (1905–1987)

Acknowledgements

I am grateful not only to my wife Thelma for all the lovely drawings in this book, but also to my father, S. I. Hsiung, for the Chinese calligraphy on the half-title page, as well as the poem on p. 194, and to Myrtle Allen for her kind permission to quote from *The Ballymaloe Cookbook.*

D-T.H.

Contents

Foreword

More than a decade has passed since I started to write the first *The Home Book of Chinese Cookery*; since then not only have I personally gained much more experience and knowledge both in cooking and writing, but the general public has become increasingly interested in eating and cooking Chinese food. For instance, when the *Home Book* was first published in 1978 very few people had even heard of the wok, let alone used one. Now it is not an exaggeration to say that the wok has become almost an everyday utensil in the British and American kitchen. I also bent over backwards to avoid including many ingredients which I thought to be too difficult to obtain, but most of these have since become widely available up and down the country. The climate is just right therefore, for a more up-to-date version of the book.

Fashions and fads in food, as in most other things, come and go: *Nouvelle Cuisine*, which got its inspiration from the Orient, and swept through the smart kitchens of Europe only a few years ago, is already on the way out. Yet Chinese cuisine, which remains practically unchanged after many centuries, has become increasingly popular in recent years. The reason for this phenomenon must be the fact that Chinese food is delicious, healthy, and on the whole economical; hence it has universal appeal.

In this completely revised and much extended edition, I have retained the spirit of the original: a cookbook based on simple yet wholesome Chinese home cooking as opposed to the professional cuisine encountered in restaurants and 'take-aways'. A number of new dishes as well as some classic traditional recipes are added. While the main structure stays unchanged, almost all the existing recipes have been rewritten – a few have even been eliminated.

Early in 1979 the Chinese phonetic alphabet known as *pinyin* officially replaced the Wade-Giles system for transliterating names of people and places. For example, Kwangtung became Guangdong and Szechuan became Sichuan. I have made the necessary adjustments in this new edition, with the exception of a few well-established names such as Peking (now Beijing), Canton (Guangzhou), and so on. And of course I absolutely refuse to change my own name from Hsiung to Xiong!

Deh-Ta Hsiung
Hampstead, London, 1986

Introduction

China is a vast country, about the same size as Western Europe or the United States; its climate and food products are similarly varied. Each region has its own specialities and different methods of cooking. But there are four areas which are generally acknowledged as the principal schools of cuisine in China: Guangdong, Huaiyang, Sichuan and Peking.

Guangdong, or Cantonese, cuisine, which most overseas Chinese restaurants claim to serve, has the widest reputation both in China and abroad, but unfortunately most people who have ventured into one of these establishments in Britain or America and ordered 'Chop suey' or 'Sweet and sour pork' may wonder why there is any fuss at all about the art of Chinese cuisine. What they do not realize is that the dishes they have sampled bear no relation whatever to the kind of fare people eat in a restaurant of similar standing in China. I shall never forget the excitement and thrill I experienced when, at about seven years old, I was taken for the very first time into a Cantonese restaurant in China where the speciality of the house was spare ribs in sweet and sour sauce – but what a sauce!

Huaiyang dishes from the Yangtze River delta are of more subtle flavour, and include various famous 'pasta' dishes such as noodles and dumplings. I wonder how many Italians are aware when they eat spaghetti or ravioli that these were first brought back from China by Marco Polo in the fourteenth century?

Food from the third region, Sichuan, by contrast, is richly flavoured and piquant. Because of its increasing popularity worldwide in recent years, I have added a number of old favourites such as 'Hot and sour soup', 'Aromatic and crispy duck' and 'Fish-flavoured aubergines'.

Finally, Peking, the capital city of China for many centuries, which as well as creating a cuisine of its own has accumulated all the best dishes from each region, and thereby become established as the culinary centre.

In this book you will find dishes from all these regions. I have selected the recipes both from my own everyday meals for the family and from those I use for entertaining, but I have included nothing which is so difficult or time-consuming that only a highly skilled professional chef could be expected to produce it.

Whether you are a good or indifferent cook in the Western sense, you should acquaint yourself with some of the principles of Chinese cooking before embarking on any recipe for Chinese food. Its taste depends far more on the method of cooking and the way it is prepared before cooking than on the natural character of the food. The Chinese attach great importance to harmony as well as contrast in selecting the various ingredients. Another thing to remember is that cooking in China is regarded as a fine art rather than an exact science; there can never be an exact measurement of ingredients, nor a precise timing for cooking a particular dish. Once you have learned the approach and a few basic techniques which are comparatively simple, the next step is experience. The details I give in the recipes are only a rough guide. After a few trials you will find a way of measuring and timing best suited to your own and your friends' tastes.

You will find that I have grouped most recipes according to ingredients and materials used rather than different methods of cooking, but I have arranged them in such a way that you can try out the simpler dishes to start off with – the more complicated and ambitious recipes come later on in the book.

You will notice that I have not mentioned any sweet courses in this book. As a rule the Chinese do not usually have any desserts to finish off a meal; they regard it as an insult to the cook if you can still eat more after a proper meal. Sweet dishes are normally eaten in between the main meals as snacks. However, for those who are used to desserts, some fresh fruit could be served as a compromise or, to be exotic, there are always such things as canned lychees, which seem to have a universal appeal.

Bon appétit!

A Few Essential Points

In the original edition of this book I said that no special tools or materials were required for cooking Chinese food. That statement is still true to a certain extent, for a Chinese cook abroad can always produce a Chinese meal, even if only locally produced ingredients are used – the 'Chineseness' of the food depends entirely on *how* it is prepared and cooked, not *what* ingredients are used. But the cook's task will be that much easier if he or she has a wok and a Chinese cleaver, the two basic implements in the Chinese *battérie de cuisine* that are considered essential if you wish to achieve the best results.

In a Western kitchen, equivalent equipment is always available: cutting knives, pots, frying pans and so on. But the Chinese cooking utensils are of an ancient design, they are made of basic and inexpensive materials, and they have been in continuous use for several thousand years and do serve a special function.

Their more sophisticated and much more expensive Western counterparts prove rather inadequate in contrast.

As for the rest of the cooking utensils, such as chopping block, stirrer, spatula, strainer, sieves, casserole and steamer, again you will find the Western versions to be less effective. Obviously there is no need for you to rush out and buy every single item I have just mentioned, but try using your existing equipment first; if you are not happy with the result, then you can go for the real thing.

o The Chinese cleaver

You will have noticed that in Chinese cooking most ingredients are cut into small pieces before they are cooked or served. The

Chinese attach great importance to the various methods of cutting. Every cookery book from China has a long chapter devoted entirely to the art of cutting – one book lists no less than forty-nine different ways of doing it using one single implement, the Chinese cleaver. A Chinese cleaver may appear to the uninitiated to be hefty and ominously sharp. But in reality it is quite light, steady, and not at all dangerous to use provided you handle it correctly and with care. Once you have learnt to regard it as a kitchen tool mainly used for cutting and *not* just a chopper, then you will be surprised how easy and simple it is to use compared with an ordinary knife. Chinese cleavers – which are *not* the same as those used in Western cooking – are available in a variety of materials and weights. Choose one made of tempered carbon steel with a wood handle. Ideally it should be neither too heavy nor too light, but a mediumweight, dual-purpose cleaver known as the 'civil and military knife' (*wen-wu dao* in Chinese). You use the lighter, front half of the blade for slicing, shredding, scoring etc; the heavier, rear half of the blade is for chopping and so on. You can also use the back of the blade as a pounder and tenderizer, and the flat side of the blade for crushing and transporting; while the end of the handle can even be used as a pestle for grinding spices etc.

Always keep your cleaver razor-sharp and clean. To prevent it rusting and getting stained, wipe it dry with a cloth or kitchen paper after use. Sharpen it frequently on a fine-grained whetstone, honing the cleaver evenly on both sides to keep the blade straight and sharp. After cleaning the blade and wiping it dry, hang the cleaver by the handle to keep the blade from becoming dulled on other metal objects in a drawer.

It is important to remember that cutting before cooking introduces harmony as well as bringing out the true flavour of the ingredients. The food should be cut into units of roughly the same shape, same size and same thickness. Thinly-cut food requires only a short cooking time, and the natural flavours are thus preserved.

The four basic cutting methods are as follows:

Slicing: the ingredients are cut into thin slices, about the size of a postage stamp, but as thin as cardboard.
Shredding: the ingredients are first cut into thin slices, stacked like a pack of playing cards, and then cut into thin strips.
Dicing: the ingredients are first cut into strips as wide as they are thick, then the strips are cut at right angles in the same width so they become small cubes.
Diagonal cutting: this method is normally used for cutting vegetables such as carrots, celery or courgettes. Roll the vegetables half a turn each time you make a diagonal cut straight down.

o Preparation and cooking methods

After cutting, the next step in preparation before actual cooking is mixing – not mixing ingredients, which comes later, but what in Chinese is called 'coating': making a paste with white of egg and cornflour then mixing in the ingredients, or mixing salt, egg white and cornflour (in that order) with meat, chicken or fish.

The various methods of cooking can be divided into four main categories: *water-cooking*, including boiling and stewing, *oil-cooking* (frying and braising), *steam-cooking*, and *fire-cooking* (roasting and barbecuing). In China the fire-cooking method is less popular for family meals, partly because most Chinese kitchens are equipped with simple stoves but no ovens. A Chinese family expects to eat fire-cooked dishes only in restaurants.

Whichever method you choose to use, the degree of heat at which you cook is most important. In China it is divided into 'military' (high or fierce) heat and 'civil' (low or gentle) heat. You must be able to control the heat with perfect ease, as it is vital that you should be able to turn it down or bring it up at the crucial moments. If the heat is too high for too long the food will be either overcooked or burnt outside and raw inside.

By far the most frequently used home-cooking method in China is quick *stir-frying*. To do this you heat up a small amount of oil in a pre-heated wok over high heat, throw in the ingredients and constantly stir and toss them for a short time. Timing here is of the utmost importance: overcooking will turn the food into a soggy mess. When correctly done, the food should be crispy and wholesome. Very little water is added, or none at all, since the high heat will bring out the natural juices from the meat and vegetables, particularly if they are fresh. This method of cooking is very economical, since the total amount of meat and vegetables required for two people is about ½ lb (225 g) of each, and it will stretch to serve four if combined with another dish. This, in the days of high food prices, is a welcome economy.

The next most popular cooking method, probably, is *braising*. You first parcook the ingredients by deep-frying, then braise them quickly in their own juice or in a little stock. Then comes *stewing*, or what we call in China *red-cooking*; the ingredients are first fried or boiled then stewed slowly in soy sauce which gives colour – hence the name.

The other frequently used methods are *deep-frying* and *steaming*. Now it is interesting to note that the whole spectrum of Chinese cooking methods can be executed in one single utensil, namely the wok.

o The wok

The wok was designed with a rounded bottom to fit snugly over a traditional Chinese brazier or oven which burns wood, charcoal or coke. It conducts and retains heat evenly, and because of the wok's shape the food always returns to the centre where the heat is most intense. For this reason it is ideally suited for quick stir-frying. When it comes to deep-frying, the conical-shaped wok requires far less oil than a flat-bottomed deep-fryer, and it has more depth (which means more heat) and more frying surface (which means more food can be cooked more quickly at one go). Furthermore, since the wok has a larger capacity at the top than at the base, when the oil level rises as the raw ingredients are added there is little chance of the oil overflowing and causing the pan to catch fire as often happens with a conventional deep-fryer.

Besides being a frying pan (deep or shallow), a wok is also used for braising, steaming, boiling and even smoking.

Just for the record, I think you should know that 'wok' is the Cantonese pronunciation of the Chinese term *huo*, which is a kind of cauldron used in ancient China. The correct transliteration is *guo*, which simply means 'pan'. The iron cooking pots and pans made during the Han dynasty (206 BC–AD 220) all show a remarkable similarity to cooking utensils of the present day, and until the twentieth century the wok changed very little for well over two thousand years!

Despite the ever-increasing interest in Chinese cookery shown by people all over the world, the average non-Chinese still cannot quite come to terms with the use of the wok except for the occasional stir-frying, and most people just seem not to be able to grasp the few fundamentals that make this utensil stand apart from all other kitchen equipment in the West. I think the explanation for this is quite simple: since the wok was originally designed to be used over a primitive brazier, its rounded bottom is not really suitable for a modern Western cooker, particularly if you cook only by electricity.

Ah, I can hear you cry, but the salesperson at the department store or wherever you bought the wok set reassured you that with the adaptor ring you should have no problem with the wok either on gas or electric cookers. Let's re-examine the whole situation.

Basically, there are only two different types of wok on the market. First there is the most commonly seen type with two handles at opposite sides. This type is usually sold as a set together with the adaptor ring, lid, ladle, spatula, steamer rack and other accessories. Then, for less than a third of the price of a set, you can buy a wok with single handle like that of a frying pan.

First, let us take a look at the double-handled wok. It is

certainly the most popular model around both in China and abroad. It is usually made of lightweight iron or steel, and the diameter ranges from 12 in (32 cm) to 18 in (46 cm). Now, unless you have a gas cooker with burners that will cradle the rounded bottom of the wok, you will have to use an adaptor ring or hob stand which will help to steady the wok when it is being used for deep-frying, braising or steaming. Personally I find the ring or stand quite a nuisance when I am using the wok for stir-frying – it never keeps still as I shake the wok about. A disadvantage of the double-handled wok is that you need strong wrists and oven gloves to lift it, as the metal handles get very hot even when they are reinforced with heat-resistant plastic or wood.

Next we will consider the single-handled wok. It may appear to be unsteady and slightly tipped to one side, but in fact it is quite safe and much easier to handle, particularly for quick stir-frying, since it offers you plenty of leverage for tilting and tossing. There is never any real danger of the whole wok tipping over as the sheer weight of the wok and of the ingredients inside help to balance it.

Those of you who have electric cookers with flat hobs should get a wok with a flat bottom. There are models made with either single or double handles, made from iron. As for woks made from stainless steel, aluminium, copper, Teflon, porcelainized enamel, with coloured exteriors and so on, all these are specifically designed and manufactured for the Western market. Not only do they always cost a great deal more than the traditional iron wok, but they are also far less efficient for the task they are supposed to perform.

Don't despair if you cannot get a good wok. For years my mother never used one. But if you decide to get one, choose an iron wok with a single handle for stir-frying and quick braising, and the double-handled version for deep-frying and steaming etc. The ideal diameter would be 14 in (36 cm) and the wok should not be too heavy to allow plenty of manoeuvrability. The depth of the wok is quite important: the extra inch or so on its vertical wall will make your stir-frying that much easier and more successful. Woks made of stainless steel or aluminium do not retain heat well, nor do they conduct the heat evenly.

There are also electric woks which all have flat bottoms inside although the exteriors are round; their main shortcomings seem to be their rather shallow sides and the fact that their maximum temperature is not quite high enough for quick stir-frying for a number of dishes. On the plus side, an electric wok frees your cooker for other use, and can even be used at the table in your dining-room. I must confess that I have been using one at home for some years now, but mainly as a second wok for braising and steaming.

To get the best out of a wok you must season and clean it properly. A new iron or steel wok is coated either with machine oil or a film of wax to keep it from rusting. This coating has to be removed and then a new coat of seasoning must be applied to the surface. The seasoning must be maintained throughout the life of the wok to keep it from rusting and to prevent food sticking to the bottom.

The best way to remove the oil or wax coating of a new wok is by burning: heat the wok over a hot stove until almost the entire surface is black, then clean it in warm, soapy water with a stiff brush and rinse well. Place the wok over a moderate heat to dry, then wipe the surface clean with a pad of kitchen paper soaked in cooking oil. The wok is now seasoned and ready for use.

After each use, wash the wok under the hot or cold water tap. *Never use detergents* as they will remove the seasoning and food will stick to the surface the next time you cook. Should any food be left sticking to the wok, scrape it off with a stiff brush or nylon scourer – don't use soap. Rinse and dry the wok thoroughly over a low heat. If the wok is not to be used again soon, rub some oil over the surface to prevent it going rusty.

When you have cooked in a new wok some eight to ten times, and if you never clean it with detergents or metal abrasives, then it will acquire a beautiful, glossy finish like a well-seasoned omelette pan. This is the patina much treasured by Chinese cooks as 'wok flavour'.

Your Store Cupboard

Traditionally, a Chinese housewife is supposed to check first thing each morning the following seven items in her kitchen: firewood, rice, oil, salt, soy sauce, vinegar and tea. A Western housewife is luckier in a way as she has no need to be bothered with the firewood problem, but she should add to this list sugar, pepper, cooking sherry and cornflour.

The following is a list of the most generally used materials and ingredients, given in alphabetical order. All these are obtainable from most Oriental stores (see below); some of the items can even be found in the delicatessen or a good supermarket.

Bamboo shoots: normally only canned ones can be bought in the West; try to get winter bamboo shoots, which are smaller and more tender than the ordinary ones. After opening the tin, drain before use; any leftovers can be stored in fresh water in a covered jar where they will keep for weeks in the refrigerator.

Bean curd: also known as *tofu*, this soft cheese-like preparation of puréed and pressed soya beans is exceptionally high in protein. It is sold in cakes about 3 in (7½ cm) square and 1 in (2½ cm) thick in Oriental and health food stores. It will keep fresh for a few days if submerged in water in a container and placed in the refrigerator. Packets of dried bean curd skins, available in sheets or sticks, will keep for a long time. The dried skin is soaked overnight in cold water, or for an hour in warm water, before use.

Bean sauce: there are basically two kinds: yellow bean sauce and black bean sauce. They are sold in cans or jars, and are sometimes called bean paste. The yellow is sweeter than the black.

Bean sprouts: use fresh bean sprouts only. Canned ones should be banned by law, since they taste nothing like the real thing. Do not bother to top and tail them, as that would take you hours to do and is quite unnecessary. Just wash, rinse and discard any husks that float on the surface of the water. They will stay fresh in a refrigerator for a few days if kept in a closed plastic bag.

Chilli bean paste: fermented bean paste mixed with hot chilli and other seasonings. Sold in jars, some are quite mild but some are very hot. You will have to try out the various brands yourself to see which one is to your taste.

Chilli sauce: very hot sauce made from chillis, vinegar, sugar and salt. It is usually sold in bottles and should be used sparingly in cooking or as a dip. Tabasco sauce can be a substitute.

Chinese dried mushrooms: you only need a very small amount in any one dish, which is just as well since they are rather expensive. Buy 4 oz (100 g) at a time; they will last you a long time and will keep indefinitely in a tightly covered jar if stored in a cool place. Soak them in cold water overnight before use, or in warm water for about 30 minutes. Fresh mushrooms, which are quite different in fragrance and texture, do not make a good substitute.

Five Spice powder: a combination of star anise, fennel, clove, cinnamon and Sichuan pepper. Use less than 1 teaspoonful at a time, as it is very pungent. It is sold in plastic bags or tins and should be stored in a tightly covered container.

Ginger root: sold by weight, fresh ginger root should be peeled, sliced and finely shredded or chopped before use. Will keep unpeeled for weeks in a dry, cool place. Alternatively, peel and place in a jar, cover with dry sherry, seal and store in the refrigerator.

Hoi Sin sauce: also known as barbecue sauce. Made from soya beans, flour, sugar, spices and red colouring. It is sold in cans or jars and will keep in the refrigerator for months.

Oyster sauce: a thickish brown sauce made from oysters and soy sauce. It is sold in bottles and will keep almost indefinitely in the refrigerator.

Rice wine: made from glutinous rice, it is also known as 'yellow wine' (*huang jiu* or *chiew* in Chinese) because of its golden amber colour. The best variety, *Shaoxing* is from the southeast of China. A good dry or medium sherry can be an acceptable substitute.

Sesame seed oil: strongly flavoured seasoning oil which is sold in bottles and keeps indefinitely. The refined yellow sesame oil sold in Middle Eastern stores is not so aromatic, has less flavour and therefore is not a very satisfactory substitute.

Sichuan peppercorns: also known as *hua chiao*, these reddish-brown peppercorns are much more aromatic, though milder, than either black or white peppercorns. They are sold in plastic bags and will keep for a long time in a tightly sealed container.

Sichuan (Szechuan) preserved vegetable: this pickled root vegetable is hot and salty. Sold in cans, once opened it can be stored in a tightly sealed jar in the refrigerator for months.

Soy sauce: sold in bottles or cans, this most popular Chinese sauce is used both for cooking and at the table. 'Light soy sauce' has more flavour than the sweeter 'dark soy sauce' which gives the food a rich, reddish colour. It will keep almost indefinitely.

Tiger lily: known as 'Yellow Flower' or 'Golden Needles' in China, it is a dried bud, golden yellow in colour. It must be soaked in water before use. Will keep indefinitely.

Water chestnuts: sold ready peeled in cans. They can be

obtained fresh during the winter months both in Britain and the USA and will keep for about a month in a refrigerator in fresh water in a covered jar.

Wooden ear: also known as 'cloud ear', it is a dried tree fungus. Only a very small amount is needed each time. Soak in warm or cold water for 20 minutes, then rinse in fresh water before use. It has a crunchy texture and a mild but subtle flavour.

o Chinese Provision Stores

There are a great number of Chinese provision stores throughout both Britain and America. In the larger cities they usually centre around a district known as Chinatown, such as Gerrard Street in London and Nelson Street in Liverpool. If you live too far from a Chinese store to shop there, write to Ken Lo's Kitchen, 14 Eccleston Street, London SW1W ONZ (01 730 7734) for an illustrated price list of items available by post.

Chopsticks and Tableware

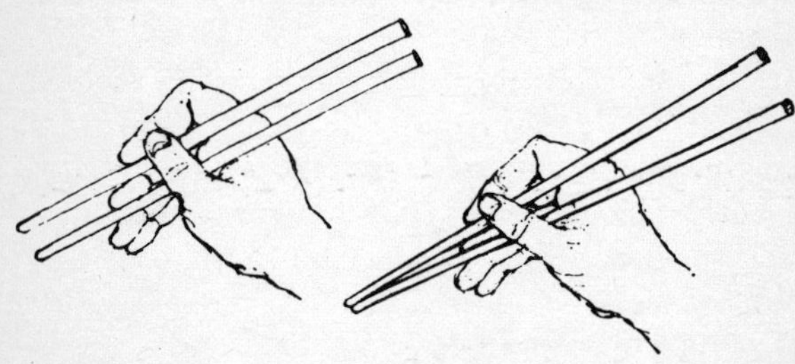

Does Chinese food taste any better when eaten with chopsticks? This is not purely an aesthetic question, but also a practical point. I think most people find it enormously satisfying to be able to use chopsticks at a Chinese table, partly because all Chinese food is prepared in such a way that it is easily picked up by chopsticks. If you regard eating with the fingers as natural, then just think of chopsticks as an extension of your fingers. Some conservative Chinese regard the Western practice of using knives and forks as barbaric – which is why some waiters in Chinese restaurants are so rude to customers who use them. Still, I myself have enjoyed eating many a meal with just a fork without too much bother.

Learning to use chopsticks is quite simple and easy – use the drawings to help you. I always maintain that using chopsticks is like riding a bicycle: you must not concentrate too hard on what you are doing, but relax and let your mind wander to other matters such as the beautiful person sitting next to you or the wonderful wine being served with the food.

At an informal Chinese meal all the dishes are brought to the table together. The host or hostess signals the start with his or her chopsticks, waving them in the air rather like the conductor of an orchestra. Then everybody picks up their chopsticks and tucks in. When you think you have had enough, you simply wave your chopsticks and mutter something like 'Please don't hurry!' But in more polite society the host and hostess constantly serve the guests, using a spoon to help them to more food from the centre of the table so that the guests never have to stretch out their arms to help themselves.

Anyway, one advantage of using Chinese tableware is that there is very little washing-up afterwards; all you need for each place setting is a medium-sized plate, a pair of chopsticks and a rice bowl, which doubles as a soup bowl when used with a porcelain spoon.

Some Useful Hints

1. Always choose the freshest vegetables you can find and do not leave them lying around too long before use. Keeping them in water may preserve the freshness of their colour, but they will still lose much of their vitamin content.
2. Always wash vegetables *before* cutting them up so that they do not lose vitamins in water.
3. Cook vegetables as soon as you have cut them, so that not too much of the vitamin content is destroyed by exposure to the air.
4. Never overcook the vegetables, and never use too much water in cooking. Do not use a lid over the pan unless specified, as this will spoil the brightness of the colour.
5. When recipes call for the use of a lid, this must be as tightly fitting as possible.
6. Do not add salt or too much soy sauce at early stages of cooking, since this will toughen the food and cause it to lose its natural flavour.
7. When frying fish, always start with high heat, then reduce to moderate. With meat, it is the other way round: start off with moderate heat then increase it for the last stage of cooking.
8. When frying chicken or shellfish, use high heat but warm oil – too hot oil will reduce the tenderness.
9. Cornflour or any form of starch, when used discreetly, will not only preserve vitamins and protein content in meats, particularly when they are finely sliced or shredded, but also retain their tenderness and delicacy. But if they are used over-generously, the food will not only look messy, it will also taste starchy.
10. Certain kinds of vegetable oils have a strong odour: if so, heat the oil with a slice of peeled ginger root before use.
11. It is easier to cut frozen meat into thin slices when still

half-frozen; but the meat should be thoroughly thawed before cooking so as not to lose its tenderness and flavour.

12. If condiments are appropriate to the dish, use them discreetly. They should enrich the flavour of the food rather than overpower it.

I

A Very Simple Meal to Begin With

Cold sliced chicken
Red-cooked beef
Boiled rice
Stir-fried pork and seasonal greens

Suggested wines:

Pouilly Fuissé or
Riesling
Beaujolais Villages or
Spanish Rioja

Having got so far, you must be keen to make a start. Whether you are cooking for the family or for close friends, you should know beforehand their likes and dislikes. One of the great advantages of Chinese cooking is that it is so flexible: even the fussiest person will normally find something to his or her liking among a choice of three or four different dishes. Another advantage is the way Chinese food 'stretches', so that an extra pair of chopsticks (or a spoon and fork) is all that you need to accommodate an unexpected guest.

As a rule, allow one dish for each person if you want a biggish meal; otherwise two dishes are ample for three or even four people. Let us assume you are cooking for six people, which is a very convenient number. Here is a suggested menu:

As a starter, serve cold sliced chicken which could be prepared beforehand. This is followed by a quick stir-fried dish, such as pork and seasonal greens which takes less than five minutes to cook (provided you have done the necessary preparation), and red-cooked beef with boiled rice (both of which should have been cooked before you start the chicken dish) – so there is very little last-minute panic even if you are a complete beginner.

Are you suitably tempted? Then let's get down to business.

Get a medium-sized young farm chicken (make sure it is fresh; frozen ones tend to be rather dry and tasteless) weighing about 2½ lb (1.1 kg). Buy ½ lb (225 g) pork fillet, which is the best, or alternatively spare rib chops, which are cheaper, or any other cut of pork that is not too fat – but on no account buy expensive pork chops. Then you will need 1½ lb (680 g) shin of beef (stewing beef is the next best). Next get ½ lb (225 g) seasonal green vegetable such as mange-touts peas, broccoli or green peppers, ¼ lb (100 g) white mushrooms, 1 lb (450 g) carrots, a bunch of spring onions (called 'scallions' in the USA), fresh ginger root and soy sauce.

That will complete your shopping list, assuming your larder has cooking oil (in China, the most commonly used cooking oil is made from vegetables such as soya beans, peanuts, rape seeds or from seeds of sunflower, camellia and cotton etc; lard or chicken fat are sometimes used, but never butter or dripping), salt, sherry (pale sherry, medium or dry is best for Chinese cooking), sugar, cornflour and rice.

Rice, as you will know, is the staple food of most Chinese. In everyday usage the Chinese words for 'rice' and 'meal' are the same, just as in English the word 'bread' is used in 'give us our daily bread' or 'bread-winner'.

o Cold sliced chicken

This is a famous Cantonese dish, also known as 'White-cut chicken'. 'White-cut' is a Chinese cooking method used for white meats that are very fresh and tender. They are cooked in large pieces in a relatively short time, then the heat is turned off and the remainder of the cooking is done by the receding heat. However, since modern cookers and Western cooking pots do not retain heat to the same extent as the traditional Chinese cooking utensils, a similar effect can be obtained by lowering the heat after the initial period of rapid boiling and then simmering gently until the required tenderness is achieved. This is the simplest dish I know and it literally requires no cooking skill whatsoever. The chicken can be cooked the night before and served the next day, or it can be cooked in the morning and served in the evening. The most important point to remember is never use a frozen chicken or an old boiler. You will need a saucepan which is large enough to hold the whole bird and which has a tightly fitting lid.

1 young farm chicken (about 2½–3 lb, 1.1–1.4 kg)
2–3 spring onions
2–3 slices ginger root
3 tablespoons Chinese rice wine or dry sherry
1 tablespoon salt

For the sauce:
2–3 tablespoons soy sauce
1 teaspoon sugar
1 tablespoon sesame seed oil
2 spring onions, finely chopped

Remove the giblets and keep them for making stock. Wash the chicken thoroughly, then place it in the saucepan with enough water to cover, add the spring onions, ginger root and rice wine or sherry, cover the pan with a tight-fitting lid and bring to the boil. Skim off the scum, add the salt, reduce the heat and simmer for 8–10 minutes only, keeping the lid very tightly shut all the time. Then remove the pan from the heat and leave to cool for 4–6 hours; the bird will continue to cook gently in the hot water provided you put something heavy on top of the lid to make sure there is no escape of heat.

About an hour before you serve it, remove the chicken and drain. (Keep the water as a base for making stock with the carcass.) If you possess a Chinese cleaver, chop the chicken into 20–24 bite-size pieces, then reassemble the bird on a dish (see p.68). Alternatively, pull the meat off the bone, cut it into small pieces and arrange them neatly on a serving dish.

Next mix the sauce with a little stock, pour it all over the chicken and serve.

o Red-cooked beef

This is basically a stew, but again it can be prepared long before you serve it; in fact, it always tastes better when warmed up and also gives you the chance to de-fat it when it has cooled.

— 1½ lb (680 g) shin of beef
3 tablespoons Chinese rice wine or sherry
2–3 slices ginger root
3 tablespoons soy sauce
1 tablespoon sugar
1 teaspoon salt
— ¾ lb (340 g) carrots

Cut the shin of beef into ½ in (12 mm) cubes. Trim off any excess fat, but leave the sinew in the meat as it gives the liquid extra flavour and richness. Put the meat in a saucepan with enough water to cover, add the rice wine or sherry and the ginger root, bring it to the boil, then let it simmer for 1 hour (needless to say with the lid on), then add the soy sauce and sugar. Continue simmering for ½ hour or so. Cut the carrots into roughly the same size pieces as the beef, add them to the stew together with the salt and cook for another 25–30 minutes before serving. The carrots will absorb some of the fat and will give the dish a contrast in colour as well as in texture.

The same method of cooking can be applied to pork or lamb, which take slightly less cooking time.

o Boiled rice

Time and again I have been asked by various people how to cook rice. The answer is very simple: you just boil with water – there is nothing more to it than that! Some people add salt to it, others drain it through a sieve or what have you; all this is quite unnecessary.

There are two main types of rice on sale in Britain: the long grain or Patna rice and the rounded or pudding rice. If you like your rice to be firm yet fluffy then use the long grain type, as the rounded rice tends to be rather soft and sticks together after cooking. Allow 2 oz (50 g) rice per person, or ¾ lb (340 g) for six (unless you are all very hearty eaters). Wash the rice in a saucepan with cold water just once, then fill the pan with more cold water so that when you put your index finger in it with the tip just touching the top of the rice, the water level just reaches the first joint of your finger. Cover with a well-fitting lid and bring to the boil. Use a spoon to give it a stir to prevent the rice sticking to the bottom of the pan when cooked. Then replace the lid tightly, turn down the heat as low as possible, and let it cook for 15–20 minutes. By then the rice is cooked but not quite ready for serving; it is best to leave it off the heat for 10 minutes or so, as (so the Chinese believe) it is bad for the digestion to eat rice that has only just been cooked.

Any leftover rice can be reheated by adding a little water, but a much nicer way of serving it is to fry it with a little oil and salt or soy sauce, together with an egg or two (see p.99).

o Stir-fried pork and seasonal greens

This is a basic recipe for cooking any meat with vegetables – usually several different kinds, according to seasonal availability. It is a very colourful dish and simple to make.

½ lb (225 g) pork fillet or spare rib chops
1 tablespoon soy sauce
1 tablespoon Chinese rice wine or sherry
1 teaspoon sugar
1 teaspoon cornflour mixed with 2 teaspoons cold water
½ lb (225 g) mange-touts peas, broccoli or green peppers
¼ lb (100 g) white mushrooms
¼ lb (100 g) carrots
1–2 spring onions, cut into short lengths
4 tablespoons oil
2 teaspoons salt

Cut the pork into thin slices about the size of an oblong postage stamp; mix with the soy sauce, the rice wine or sherry, the sugar and the cornflour-and-water paste. Leave the meat to marinate while the vegetables are washed and prepared.

If the mange-touts are young and tender, they will not be stringy and need only be topped and tailed; snap older, larger ones in half. Cut the rest of the vegetables into thin slices about the same size as the pork.

All this could be done before the guests arrive. So after you have served the cold sliced chicken as a starter, you now go into the kitchen to cook this pork and vegetable dish which, as I have said, should take no more than 5 minutes in all.

Heat up the wok or a large frying pan first until very hot, then add about 2 tablespoons of oil, wait for it to smoke (this will take about ¾ minute), then reduce the heat and let the oil cool down a little, meanwhile swirling it to cover most of the surface of the wok. Add the meat and stir-fry it by constantly turning the meat until each slice is covered with the heated oil. This should take no longer than 1 minute, otherwise the meat will be overcooked. Remove the meat with a perforated spoon and put it back in the mixing bowl. Now, if you have used a well-seasoned wok or pan and have heated it up to a high temperature before pouring in the oil, then there should be no need for you to clean it at this stage. Just increase the heat to high again and reheat the wok, add the remaining oil and wait for it to smoke (this will take about 1 minute). Toss in the spring onions to flavour the oil and stir for a second or two, but before they turn brown quickly add the vegetables – carrots and greens should go in first, followed by the mushrooms. When the wet vegetables meet the hot oil they will make a rather loud noise, but do not be alarmed; just stir vigorously so that all the bits and pieces are covered with oil. Continue stirring for about ½ minute, add the salt and stir for a few seconds more, then add the partly cooked pork. Cook the pork and vegetables together for 1 minute longer, stirring all the time. At this point the ingredients should have produced enough natural juices to form a sort of gravy, but if the contents of the pan are too dry and start to burn, add a little stock or water and bring it to the boil before serving. The pork should taste succulent and tender, and the vegetables should be crisp with a bright and shiny appearance.

This is the basic method of stir-frying almost any food in China. Once you have mastered it there is no end to the variations you can create by using different combinations of meats and vegetables. The two most important things to remember here are heat and timing, particularly the latter as sometimes even a fraction of a second can make all the difference. As you can see from the above instructions, the exact timing is closely related to the degree of heat, which is why it is impossible to give a precise figure; much depends on the type of stove or the thickness of the pan you use. Therefore what I can give you can only be a rough guide. Also, as it is imperative that you should not take your eyes off the pan while cooking, let alone stare at the second hand of a clock or watch, you should really learn to time your cooking by the appearance and sound – yes, sound. Remember what I said earlier: when you first throw the ingredients into hot oil they will make a loud noise, but as you continue cooking the noise will gradually become subdued – usually the sign that they are almost done. I suggest that just to start with you have someone standing by with a watch that shows the seconds to call out every 10 seconds or so.

As far as I know, no cook in China ever used a clock to time their cooking – or any measure for their ingredients either. What they usually do is to taste a bit from the pan while still cooking to see if it is nearly done, or if any more salt or whatever is needed. For it is comparatively simple to adjust seasonings and continue cooking a little longer if necessary, but it would be too late if too much seasoning had been used already or the food had been overcooked!

So now you have cooked your first Chinese meal. I am sure you have enjoyed preparing it and your guests and family have probably enjoyed eating it. If they are used to the 'chop suey' type of Chinese food, they should have been pleasantly surprised to discover the home cooking of China.

Incidentally, if you are cooking for only four people, then by all means omit one of the dishes such as the cold sliced chicken or red-cooked beef; as for the stir-fried pork and seasonal greens, you can easily leave out the pork, cook just the vegetables and serve as a side dish.

A Chinese meal is served absolutely ready to eat – there is no last-minute carving on the table, no dishing out separate items such as meat, vegetables, gravy or sauce, with all the attendant condiments. There is no long prelude when you all wait for everybody to be served before you start. At a Chinese table, when everyone is seated, the host will raise his chopsticks and say '*Chin-chin*' ('Please-please') – and then you all pick up your chopsticks and enjoy yourselves.

The enjoyment of the meal would be enormously enhanced if you served wine or wines with it: as the saying goes, 'Wine makes any meal into a feast'. The subject of drinking wine with Chinese food is dealt with in Chapter X, but a few words about what to drink with this, your first Chinese meal, are appropriate here.

Contrary to common belief in the West, tea is seldom served at mealtimes in China. It is true that tea is the most popular beverage of most Chinese, but it is drunk before or after a meal, or indeed during any other time of the day; at everyday lunches or suppers soup is usually served throughout the meal, and for more formal occasions or when entertaining wines and spirits are essential parts of the fare.

To start with, an inexpensive dry white wine such as Pouilly Fuissé or a less dry hock – or any white wine made from Riesling – will serve both as an apéritif and as an accompaniment to the cold chicken. Of course if it happens to be somebody's birthday or any other celebration, champagne would be ideal, and so would a good sparkling wine – but one that is not too sweet.

A light red wine will go best with the beef and pork dishes. Here the scope is very wide, much depending on your personal taste and, of course, your pocket. As a guide, choose something which is not too heavy or sweet. A young, fresh Beaujolais would be most suitable, otherwise a good claret or Côtes du Rhône, or any Provençal wine that carries a VDQS label.

II

A Great Leap Forward

Fried beef and tomatoes
Soy-braised chicken
Lions' heads (pork meat balls)
Pork and mushroom soup
Stir-fried prawns and peas

See also:
Boiled rice (p.28)

Suggested wines:

Mâcon blanc or
Californian Chardonnay
Mâcon rouge or
Bourgogne (Pinot Noir)
St Emilion or
Spanish Rioja

If I have sufficiently whetted your appetite in the previous chapter, you must be very keen to get on to the next stage and try out some slightly more complicated recipes.

This time let us take a great leap forward by cooking for eight to ten people, for whom you will need at least five dishes including a soup.

As you will see from the recipes listed, this is a well-balanced menu which consists of what we in China call the three 'meats' – pork, chicken and fish. These are supplemented by other ingredients to give a contrast not only in tastes but also in colours and textures.

Quite a few hours' preparation beforehand is required, and careful planning for the operation will avoid last-minute panic in the kitchen after the guests have arrived. But experience must have told you that no good food can come out of the kitchen without some hard work! I hope you will agree that this menu sounds very exciting and therefore is worth a little bit of extra trouble both to please yourself and your guests. Let's say it will be a challenge to test yourself and your skill, for if you can do these dishes well then I assure you that nothing in this book is beyond your capability.

First, the shopping list:

½ lb (225 g) peeled prawns (or uncooked, unshelled prawns if you can get them from a good fishmonger)
1 young farm chicken (2½–3 lb, 1.1–1.4 kg)
¾ lb (340 g) frying beef steak

- 2 lb (900 g) minced pork (weight exclusive of bones). If you have a mincer at home, then just get this amount of pork, either spare rib chops or any other cheaper cuts such as blade bone or hand (called shoulder butt or picnic shoulder in the USA); otherwise ask the butcher to mince most of the pork for you, but take the bones too, and a small unminced piece of lean pork about ½ lb (225 g) in weight
- ½ lb (225 g) peas (fresh or frozen, preferably petits pois)
- ¾ lb (340 g) hard tomatoes (under- rather than over-ripe)
- ½ lb (225 g) mushrooms
- 1 lettuce
- 1 medium-sized cabbage (about 1½ lb, 680 g); ideally a Chinese cabbage, also called Chinese leaves or celery cabbage, otherwise a green or white cabbage
- 1 bunch spring onions
- fresh ginger root
- Sichuan peppercorns or *hua chiao*

Needless to say, you will also need oil, salt, soy sauce, sugar, cornflour, sherry, eggs and rice.

o Soy-braised chicken

This dish can be prepared the day before and eaten cold, but it is nicer served on the same day it is cooked.

- 1 fresh farm chicken (3–3½ lb, 1.4–1.6 kg)
- 1 tablespoon freshly ground Sichuan pepper (black or white peppers can be used instead)
- 1–2 tablespoons finely minced fresh ginger root
- 5 tablespoons soy sauce (3 of light and 2 of dark if possible)
- 3 tablespoons sherry
- 1 tablespoon brown sugar
- 3 tablespoons oil
- 1 lettuce
- Radishes or tomatoes for garnish (optional)

Wash the chicken and dry it thoroughly (use the giblets for other recipes, see p.39), then rub both inside and out with freshly ground pepper and finely minced ginger root (dried ginger powder should not be used). Marinate the bird with the soy sauce, sherry and sugar in a deep bowl for at least 3 hours, turning it over now and then.

At this stage, you should start preparing other dishes, but when you return to cook the chicken, heat the oil in a pre-heated wok or large saucepan, take the chicken out of the marinade and brown it lightly all over, then add the marinade diluted with about 1 pint (600 ml) water. Bring it to the boil, reduce the heat, and simmer gently for 40–45 minutes under cover, turning it over 3–4 times but taking care not to break the skin.

To serve, remove the chicken from the wok or pan and let it cool down a little before chopping it into bite-size pieces (see p.68). Arrange them neatly on a bed of lettuce leaves, then pour over a couple of tablespoons of the sauce. To add colour, you can decorate the edge of the plate with radishes or tomatoes. The remains of the sauce could be stored in the refrigerator almost indefinitely, and can be used for making a wonderful egg dish (see recipe on p.56). You could serve this chicken dish cold as a starter or as a part of the main course. It would certainly make an ideal buffet-style meal.

o Lions' heads

One of the unusual aspects of Chinese food is the fascinating names given to most dishes. In order not to alarm any of your guests who might be squeamish, you had better explain that the pork meat balls are supposed to resemble the shape of lions' heads and the cabbage is supposed to look like the mane, hence the name. When my daughter Kai-lu was a little girl and was offered this dish for the first time, she absolutely refused to touch it, as she had been to the zoo earlier in the day. Later it became her favourite dish, so much so that she didn't allow that there could be a proper Chinese meal without it.

2 lb (900 g) pork
1–2 spring onions, finely chopped
1 teaspoon finely chopped fresh ginger root, peeled
2–3 mushrooms (optional)
a few prawns (optional)
2 tablespoons sherry
2 tablespoons light soy sauce
2 teaspoons sugar
1 egg
1 tablespoon cornflour
about 3–4 tablespoons oil
1½ lb (680 g) cabbage
1 teaspoon salt

You could start making this dish the day before if you like, but I think it always tastes slightly better when not reheated. Allow yourself about 3 hours on the day it is to be served.

First bone the pork if it hasn't been done already, and use the bones to make a stock for the basis of the soup (see p.39). If you brought home the pork in a whole piece, then keep aside a small lean piece for the soup later. Now coarsely mince the pork with its fat, mix it thoroughly with finely chopped spring onions and ginger root, add finely chopped mushrooms and prawns (if using), together with sherry, soy sauce, sugar, the lightly beaten egg, and finally, cornflour. Shape the meat into 4 large round balls and put them aside.

At this point, you can get on with the preparation of other dishes. When you are ready to cook the lions' heads, heat the oil in a largish saucepan or casserole. While you wait for it to get hot, quickly cut the cabbage in quarters lengthwise (or in 6–8 segments if it is a round cabbage), add to the pot with salt and stir to make sure that all sides of the cabbage are coated with oil, then place the meat balls on top and add enough stock or water just to cover the cabbage. Bring to the boil, then put on the lid and simmer gently for 30 minutes. Alternatively, you can cook the casserole in the oven for 1 hour at 350°F(180°C), gas mark 4.

You can serve the dish from the casserole or, if cooked in a saucepan, transfer the cabbage to a large bowl with the meat balls arranged on top. It is always served with rice as a main course of the meal, never as a starter. In fact if you are cooking for three or four people only, this dish will be ample just by itself.

o Pork and mushroom soup

Chinese soups are mostly a clear broth to which vegetables or meats or both are added just before serving. When stock is not available, as often is the case, a Chinese housewife simply stir-fries a small amount of greens, then adds some water and soy sauce, brings it rapidly to the boil and serves it in a bowl throughout the meal.

pork bones
chicken giblets (if available)
1 small piece fresh ginger root
2–3 spring onions
½ lb (225 g) pork
1 tablespoon soy sauce
½ lb (225 g) mushrooms
salt and pepper to taste

Place the pork bones and chicken giblets in a saucepan, add about 3 pt (1.7 litres) cold water together with a small piece unpeeled ginger and 1–2 spring onions, bring it to the boil then reduce heat and let it simmer under cover for at least 1½ hours, then strain through a fine sieve – you should end up with about 2 pt (1 litre) good stock.

Thinly slice the pork kept aside from the lions' heads, marinate with a little soy sauce. Wash the mushrooms and cut them into thin slices lengthwise.

Bring the strained stock to a rolling boil, add the pork and mushrooms; boil rapidly for a few seconds. Then place a finely chopped spring onion and seasonings (a little salt or soy sauce) in a large serving bowl, pour the boiling soup over it and stir well.

Serve hot.

Stir-fried prawns and peas

This is a very colourful dish, which makes an excellent starter. It is very simple to make, and most of the preparations can be done long before so that it only requires a minimum cooking time.

½ lb (225 g) prawns
4 egggs
1 teaspoon cornflour blended with 2 teaspoons cold water
1–2 spring onions, finely chopped
3–4 tablespoons oil
½ lb (225 g) peas
1 teaspoon salt
1 tablespoon dry sherry

Wash the prawns before shelling, dry them thoroughly, then use a sharp knife to make a shallow incision down the back of each prawn and pull out the black intestinal vein. If the prawns are large, then split each one in half lengthwise, then cut into small pieces; smaller prawns can be left whole.

Mix the prawns with about half an egg white and the cornflour, blend well with your fingers.

Lightly beat the eggs with a pinch of salt and a few bits of finely chopped spring onions, scramble the mixture over a moderate heat in a little hot oil, then remove and put it aside.

Just before serving this dish, heat about 3 tablespoons oil in a pre-heated wok or frying pan over high heat, stir-fry the peas for about ½ minute, then add the prawns and continue stirring for another minute or so. Sprinkle with the salt and sherry and stir a few more times before adding the scrambled eggs. Blend everything together well. Finally, garnish with the finely chopped spring onions and serve hot.

Fried beef and tomatoes

Pork is definitely the most popular meat in China, but we have about four million Muslims plus about twice that number of other smaller ethnic groups who eat beef and mutton to the exclusion of pork.

As a child, I was told not to eat beef for humanitarian reasons: for centuries oxen and water buffalo were traditionally the symbol of cultivation and it would be too crude to eat the flesh of the animal which helped to feed us. My grandfather, who was a classical scholar of his time, always refused on principle to touch a beef dish. Once I watched him enjoying one at a banquet, but he insisted afterwards that he didn't know what he was eating at the time. My nanny, who was an excellent cook herself, maintained that she could tell the difference between beef and any other meat from a mile off, and consequently she had a strong dislike of cooking beef in her kitchen, let alone eating it.

Years later, I discovered that beef was fairly widely eaten by the Cantonese and Sichuanese, though they tend to treat it as rather inferior to pork or chicken – which is not hard to understand since by the time the poor beast had done a long life's hard work, its meat would be too tough and tasteless, and great efforts would be required to render it palatable. This is why most Chinese recipes for beef call for the use of bicarbonate of soda in the marinade to tenderize the meat. This is quite unnecessary in the West, as the quality of the beef is much superior, and the meat is usually well hung which is never the case in China.

Again this is a very simple dish to make. If you have done all the preparation beforehand, then the actual cooking time should be no more than 3 minutes at the very most.

¾ lb (340 g) frying beef
1 teaspoon sugar
1 tablespoon soy sauce
2 tablespoons dry sherry
1 teaspoon cornflour
¾ lb (340 g) tomatoes
1–2 spring onions
1–2 thin slices fresh ginger root
4 tablespoons oil

1 teaspoon salt
freshly ground pepper

Trim all the excess fat off the meat with a sharp knife, then cut it into as thin slices as possible across the grain. Mix it with sugar, soy sauce, sherry and cornflour and leave it to marinate for at least 30 minutes.

Cut the tomatoes into ¼ in (6 mm) thick slices – do not peel off the skin, which has all the goodness in it. Cut the spring onions and ginger root into small pieces. Then all is ready for the final operation.

Heat a wok or frying pan over a high heat until very hot, add the oil, wait for it to smoke then add the beef and stir vigorously to prevent it from sticking to the pan and to make sure the pieces are not stuck together. As soon as the colour of the meat changes from dark to pale – this will take only about 30 seconds if you keep the heat high – quickly scoop it out with a perforated spoon. There should still be enough oil left in the pan (if not, add a little more) to fry the tomatoes with spring onions and ginger root; stir for a few seconds before adding the partly cooked beef to the pan. Cook together for about 20–30 seconds, stirring constantly. Now add salt and pepper, stir a few times more, and it is ready.

Serve it while it is still sizzling hot. The beef should taste so tender that it melts in the mouth, and the tomato, if you have managed to get some half-ripe hard ones, should be crisp and crunchy. Just picture the colours on the table when you serve this dish side by side with the stir-fried prawns and peas – one brown and red, the other pink, green and yellow. You just couldn't fail to win admiration from your guests!

There are several ways of serving this meal. First, the informal, homely way in which you serve all the dishes, including soup and rice, all together, which means you make the soup first, keeping it warm while quickly stir-frying the two dishes one immediately after the other (you can save a lot of time if you pre-heat enough oil for both dishes before the actual cooking, so that you don't have to wait too long in between for the oil to reach the required temperature). You then serve them with the chicken and lions' heads with rice, all of which should have been ready cooked beforehand. This way the host or hostess, who these days is usually the cook, can stay at the table throughout the meal and does not have to rush out to the kitchen in between courses.

Second, there is the Western way in which you have the soup first, then return to the kitchen to cook the two stir-fried dishes and serve all the rest. Only after that can the cook relax and enjoy the meal with his or her guests.

The third, and traditionally the correct, way and therefore more formal, is to serve the soy-braised chicken on its own and as a cold starter, followed by the two stir-fried dishes either one after another or together as hot starters; then the soup which is supposed to clear your palate for the main course, which in this case is lions' heads served with rice. Some people may find this rather strange, but I can assure you that it is very sound logic; only it is a little hard on the cook who has to jump up several times between the courses.

Now about wine. This meal definitely calls for more than two different wines, so whichever way you choose to serve the meal, I would suggest one white and two red as the safest bet. The white could be a sparkling one, which is all right for the prawn dish but not ideal for the beef, so a better choice would be something which has not only got body but also bite. In the original edition of this book (I was writing in the early 1970s), I recommended a Meursault or Montrachet! Now, as you know the price of good quality burgundy has since soared so high that it is way beyond reach for us ordinary mortals. To be more realistic, why not try a Mâcon blanc or Mâcon-Villages or Mâcon followed by the name of a commune; the two best known are Lugny and Vire. Apart from the fact that these wines are usually good value, their flowery aroma and fruity taste with a refreshing acidity make them an ideal accompaniment for a number of Chinese dishes. Do not overlook the much undervalued Californian Chardonnay either, some can almost match a great white burgundy.

Again, the scope for red wine is wide. The only thing to remember is the general rule: white before red; young before old; dry before sweet and, of course, lesser wine before a great one. '*Fay ce que vouldras*', said Rabelais more than four hundred years ago; it is still true today. The main reason why we drink wine is for sheer enjoyment; if you become too inhibited about it, then why bother? It goes without saying that your enjoyment will vary according to the occasion or setting as well as the company you are drinking with. But it is just as well to bear in mind that a claret served with seafood will taste rather metallic and thus spoil both the food and wine, while a good hock will be wasted on richly flavoured beef dish. But pork and chicken are quite another matter: they are both so versatile that almost any wine, red or white, can taste good with them. The only thing to remember here is that if a certain dish has a pungent seasoning such as ginger, chilli, star anise or sesame seed oil, then save your finest bottle of wine for something less spiced. Since the wine's elegance and flavour are to be overwhelmed, there is hardly any point in wasting money on specially good wine.

Luckily for this particular meal, neither the soy-braised chicken nor the lions' heads are strongly spiced, so you can literally serve any wine you like with them, provided they are good enough to do justice to your cooking. If you have started the meal with a Mâcon blanc, then it is only natural that you would follow it with Mâcon Rouge or Bourgogne, both of which have a good deal of fruit and, although never very smooth, go well with almost all types of Chinese food. For the claret lovers, you might like to serve a St Emilion or Pomerol. Of course a good Spanish Rioja is beautifully aromatic and delicious as well as being wonderful value.

There are, of course, many other wines you might choose to serve – so many that I have devoted a whole chapter to the subject at the end of this book.

III

Soups and Starters

Soups
Basic stock
Egg-flower soup
Bean curd and spinach soup
Meat and vegetable soup
Hot and sour soup
West Lake beef soup
Fish slices soup
Lamb and cucumber soup
San-xian (three-delicacies) soup

See also:
Pork and mushroom soup (p.39)
Long-simmered whole chicken (p.85)
Fish-head soup (p.165)
Duck soup (p.177)

Starters
Chinese cabbage salad
Sweet and sour cucumber
Pickled radishes
Braised eggs
Fragrant pork
Crystal-boiled pork
'Agitated' kidney flowers
Braised tripe
'Smoked' fish
Phoenix-tail prawns
'Agitated' prawns

See also:
Cold sliced chicken (p.26)
Soy-braised chicken (p.36)
Sliced chicken with ham and broccoli (p.82)
Hot and sour cabbage (p.91)
Prawns in shells (p.160)
Sesame seed prawn toast (p.160)
Gold and silver duck (p.171)
Duck liver in wine sauce (p.172)
Braised duck (p.174)
Roast duck Canton-style (p.174)

Let's assume you have sailed through your big test with triumph. This must have given you a lot of self confidence as well as the urge to carry on with more exciting dishes. But before we go any further, I ought to caution you not to get over-confident about it. True enough, I did say that if you could do these dishes well, then nothing is beyond your capability. But you cannot expect to master the art of Chinese cuisine overnight, for it requires a lot of experience and practice with not just a few dishes cooked in the simple way but with literally dozens of different methods and ingredients. So before we embark on more elaborate fare, let's get down to a few more basic recipes that are simple to prepare and easy to cook.

As mentioned on p.32, a simply made soup is usually served throughout an everyday meal in China. It is meant to act as a lubricant to help wash down the bulky and savoury foods, since we do not have the habit of drinking water with our meals (nor do we drink tea with food either, except for a small minority of people in certain parts of China).

There is no need for you to break the Western tradition of

serving soup at the beginning of your meal, therefore we shall start at the very beginning:

○ Basic stock

The very first item a Chinese cook would prepare when starting work in the kitchen each morning is a good stock which is used for cooking throughout the day when required, and is the basis for soup making as well. Any leftovers at the end of the day can be refrigerated and kept for up to 4–5 days; alternatively it can be frozen in small containers and an amount defrosted as required.

1½–2 lb (680–900 g) chicken pieces
1–1½ lb (450–680 g) pork spare ribs or bones
1 large piece fresh ginger root
3–4 spring onions
8 pints (4.5 litres) water
3–4 tablespoons Chinese rice wine or dry sherry

Trim off excess fat from the chicken and pork, place them together with ginger root, unpeeled but cut into chunks, and spring onions in a large saucepan or pot, add the water and bring to the boil. Skim off the scum, then reduce the heat but keep it on the boil, uncovered, for at least 1½ hours; by then you should end up with about 6 pints (3.5 litres) good stock.

Strain the stock, add the wine and bring it back to the boil again. Simmer for 5 minutes or so, then it is ready to be used for cooking or as the basis for soup. Both the chicken and pork have given up their flavour to the stock during the long cooking; not even our cats would give the meat a second glance, therefore there is not much point in keeping it.

Allow ⅔ cup (approx. 6 fluid oz or 175 ml) stock per person when making soup; therefore 1 pint (600 ml) will serve four or more with the addition of other ingredients.

Soups

Egg-flower soup

If stock is not available, a chicken stock cube dissolved in water may be used as substitute but it will have a quite different flavour. Remember to reduce the amount of soy sauce at least by half if you are using a stock cube.

1 pint (600 ml) good stock
1–2 eggs
1 teaspoon salt
1 tablespoon light soy sauce
1 spring onion, finely chopped

Bring the stock to the boil. Lightly beat the eggs with a pinch of salt. Pour in the beaten eggs very slowly while stirring the stock. Add the seasonings and garnish with spring onions. Serve hot.

Bean curd and spinach soup

This is a very colourful and delicious soup. When spinach is not in season, you can substitute lettuce or watercress.

1 cake bean curd (tofu)
¼ lb (100 g) spinach leaves (weight exclusive of stems)
1 pint (600 ml) good stock
1 teaspoon salt
1 tablespoon light soy sauce

Cut the bean curd into 12 small slices about ¼ in (0.5 cm) thick. Wash the spinach leaves. If they are large, cut them into pieces not much bigger than the size of a matchbox.

Bring the stock to the boil over high heat, add the bean curd and spinach and simmer for about 2 minutes (lettuce or watercress require much less cooking time). Skim the surface to make it clear, add seasonings, and stir well.

Serve hot.

o Meat and vegetable soup

This is a variation of the Pork and mushroom soup recipe on p.39. For meat you can use pork, beef, chicken, liver or kidney; for vegetable you can use spinach, Chinese leaves, green cabbage, mange-touts peas, lettuce or watercress.

¼ lb (100 g) lean pork
1 tablespoon Chinese rice wine or dry sherry
1 tablespoon light soy sauce
¼ lb green vegetable
1 pint (600 ml) good stock
1 teaspoon salt

Thinly slice the meat, marinate with the rice wine or sherry and a little soy sauce for about 10 minutes.

Wash the vegetable and cut into 1 in (2.5 cm) lengths.

Bring the stock to the boil, add the meat slices and stir to separate them. Boil for 30 seconds only, then remove the meat with a strainer or sieve.

Skim the soup, then add the vegetable and cook for about 1–1½ minutes depending on the type of greens used. (Chinese leaves, green cabbage will require about 2 minutes cooking time, while spinach and mange-touts peas need only 1½ minutes, and lettuce and watercress should not be cooked for more than ½ minute at the very most.) Place the meat with seasonings in a serving bowl, pour the soup over it, stir well and serve hot.

o Hot and sour soup

This is an old favourite for most people who frequent Peking and Sichuan restaurants. It is one of the few Chinese thick soups. There are a number of different recipes, but they are all made hot and sour by the addition of vinegar and plenty of freshly ground pepper.

¼ lb (100 g) pork or chicken
1 cake bean curd

3–4 Chinese dried mushrooms, soaked
1 pint (600 ml) stock
1 tablespoon rice wine or sherry
1 tablespoon soy sauce
1 teaspoon white pepper
1 tablespoon vinegar
1 teaspoon salt
1 tablespoon cornflour

Thinly shred the pork, bean curd and the mushrooms. Bring the stock to a rolling boil, add the pork, bean curd and mushrooms, simmer for 2–3 minutes, then add wine, soy sauce, pepper, vinegar and salt. Now blend the cornflour with a little cold water to make a smooth paste, pour into the soup slowly, stirring all the time. Serve as soon as the soup thickens.

A small amount of finely shredded bamboo shoots and a lightly beaten egg may be added to the soup in order to make it into an even thicker and more substantial dish.

o West Lake beef soup

This is a popular Cantonese recipe, and for years I just couldn't understand why it was named after a famous lake in the scenic city of Hangzhou in Eastern China. Then only recently I discovered that there is also a beauty spot in Canton called West Lake. So the mystery is solved at last!

¼ lb (100 g) beef steak
1 teaspoon salt
1 teaspoon sugar
1 tablespoon soy sauce
1 tablespoon Chinese rice wine or dry sherry
2 tablespoons cornflour
a few drops of sesame seed oil
1 pt (600 ml) stock
1 egg, lightly beaten

¼ lb (100 g) green peas
1 spring onion, finely chopped

Coarsely chop the beef steak into small pieces – not quite as small as mince. Now mix the beef with a pinch of salt, about ½ teaspoon sugar, ½ tablespoon each of soy sauce and wine, about 1 teaspoon cornflour blended with a little cold water, and a few drops of sesame seed oil. Marinate for at least 30 minutes.

To make the soup (this is best done just before serving), bring the stock to the boil, then pour in the beaten egg stirring the soup constantly, add the peas together with the remains of the seasonings, bring to the boil again, add the beef and thicken the soup with the cornflour and water mixture. Garnish with finely chopped spring onion and serve hot. Adjust seasonings (salt and pepper) if necessary.

o Fish slices soup

Ideally use the fillet of a flatfish such as lemon sole or plaice. It is not necessary to remove the skin, which helps to keep the flesh of the fish together when cooked.

½ lb (225 g) fish fillet (lemon sole or plaice)
½ egg white, lightly beaten
2 teaspoons cornflour
1 pint (600 ml) chicken and/or meat stock (p.48)
1 tablespoon light soy sauce
1 lettuce heart or watercress
1 spring onion, finely chopped
salt and pepper to taste

Cut the fish into large slices (about the size of a matchbox), mix with the egg white and the cornflour blended with a little cold water.

Bring the stock to the boil, add the fish slices one at a time, and simmer for about 1 minute with soy sauce. Meanwhile thinly shred the lettuce heart (if using watercress, just wash and trim) and add to the soup together with the finely chopped spring onions; adjust seasonings and serve immediately.

Lamb and cucumber soup

This is a variation of the hot and sour soup (p.50), but much simpler to prepare and equally delicious – if not even more so!

½ lb (225 g) leg of lamb fillet
1 tablespoon Chinese rice wine or dry sherry
1 tablespoon soy sauce
1 teaspoon sesame seed oil
½ cucumber
1 pint (600 ml) good stock
salt and pepper to taste
about 2 teaspoons vinegar (more if so desired)

Cut the lamb into very thin slices about the size of a large postage stamp. Marinate with wine, soy sauce and sesame seed oil for 10–15 minutes. Thinly slice the cucumber into similar size; do not peel.

Bring the stock to the boil, add the lamb slices and seasonings together with cucumber and bring to the boil once more. Simmer for about 1 minute at the very most. Overcooking will toughen the meat particularly if it is cut very thinly. Serve hot.

San-xian (three-delicacies) soup

It is interesting to note that the Chinese character *xian* (delicious) is a compound word made up of *yu* (fish) and *yang* (sheep) – the Chinese seem to have discovered long ago that the combination of fish and meat produces a perfect balance of flavours. This soup has gone one stage further by adding a third delicacy – chicken. What more can you ask for?

¼ lb (100 g) peeled prawns (or scallops, crab meat, oyster etc)
¼ lb (100 g) honey-roast ham

¼ lb (100 g) chicken breast meat, skinned and boned
1½ pints (850 ml) stock
1 teaspoon salt
1 spring onion, finely chopped
fresh coriander leaves or parsley to garnish

Ideally you should use uncooked prawns; if you can't get them use ready-cooked prawns and add them to the soup very last – even after the salt.

Thinly slice the ham and chicken meat into small pieces. If the prawns are large, then cut them into 2 or 3 pieces each.

Bring the stock to the boil, add the chicken, ham and prawns, bring back to the boil once more, add salt, and simmer for about 1 minute at the very most, then add the spring onions. Serve hot with garnish.

• Starters

Some of you may not know that in China we have an immense variety of dishes that are traditionally served at the beginning of a meal as starters just like hors d'oeuvre or antipasta in the West. These dishes are generally small and simple, and are usually served cold; but for a special occasion or at a formal dinner they can be quite elaborate and even spectacular (obviously we are not concerned with those in a book on home cooking).

One of the advantages of these dishes is that most, if not all, of them can be prepared and cooked well in advance – hours or even days before. Another point to bear in mind is that if some of these dishes are cooked in fairly large quantity, then any leftovers can be served again on another occasion, either alone or in combination with other dishes. Of course, some of these dishes are ideal for buffet-style meals or party food.

○ Chinese cabbage salad

Traditionally, the Chinese seldom eat raw vegetables, partly for hygienic reasons since manure has been extensively used as fertilizer in vegetable gardening. Most so-called 'salads' in Chinese cooking are in effect ingredients lightly cooked (usually by blanching) then served cold with a special dressing. Vegetables grown in the West and by modern methods can be served raw quite safely.

1 small Chinese cabbage (sometimes known as Chinese leaves)
1 small green pepper
1 small red pepper

For the salad dressing:
1 teaspoon salt
1 teaspoon sugar
1 tablespoon light soy sauce
2 teaspoons sesame seed oil

Remove the tough outer leaves of the cabbage, wash and dry the inner leaves and heart, then cut each leaf into large slices and place them in a serving bowl.

Seed and core the green and red peppers and thinly slice them diagonally. Place them on top of the cabbage.

Sprinkle the salt and sugar evenly all over the salad and leave it to stand for a few minutes. Finally, add the soy sauce and sesame seed oil, bring the bowl to the table, and toss and mix the salad just before serving.

o Sweet and sour cucumber

Cucumbers have been widely cultivated in China for more than two thousand years since their introduction from India where they originated. There are a number of species on the market, the most common being dark green with a smooth skin and about 1 ft (300 mm) in length. This vegetable, although very watery, is eaten cooked as well as raw in China.

1 medium-sized cucumber
1 teaspoon salt

1 tablespoon sugar
1 tablespoon vinegar
a few drops sesame seed oil

Split the cucumber in half lengthways, then cut it across into thick chunks. Do not peel, but extract its bitterness by marinating it with the salt for 10 minutes or so, then pouring the juice away. After that, mix it with sugar and vinegar, garnish with a few drops of sesame seed oil, and it is ready to serve.

Pickled radishes

These radishes can either be served on their own, or they can be used as decorative garnishes for other dishes.

2 bunches large radishes
1 teaspoon salt
2–3 teaspoons sugar

Choose radishes that are roughly equal in size if you possibly can, and discard the stalks and tails. Wash in cold water and dry well.

Use a sharp knife to make many cuts as close to each other as possible on each of the radishes about two-thirds of the way down, but not all the way through.

Put the radishes in a large jar. Add salt and sugar, shake the jar well so that each radish is coated with the mixture. Leave to marinate for several hours or overnight. Just before serving, pour off the liquid and spread out each radish like a fan. Arrange the radishes either on a plate on their own or along the edge of a plate that contains other food.

Braised eggs

If you have tried out the recipes for soy-braised chicken (p.36) or fragrant pork (p.57), then you should have some sauce left stored in the refrigerator. The best result for this egg dish would be to use a mixture of more than one of these sauces; otherwise any one of them will do.

6 eggs
sauce to cover (see pp.36, 57)

The method is very simple. All you have to do is to hard-boil 6 eggs in water for 5 minutes or so, then carefully remove the shells and simmer them in the sauce over a gentle heat for 15–20 minutes, turning the eggs over now and again if there is not enough sauce to cover them all completely.

Turn off the heat and leave the eggs to cool in the sauce, for say 2–3 hours. Just before serving, take them out and cut them into halves or quarters. Arrange them on a plate either on a bed of lettuce or decorated with pickled radishes.

o Fragrant pork

Among the cheapest cuts of meat on the market is belly pork (called bacon piece in the USA). In China it is known as 'five flowers meat' because when viewed in cross-section the alternate layers of fat and meat form a pretty pink and white pattern. If you cook this dish in a fairly large quantity it can be served at a number of meals, or the leftovers can be used in other dishes such as Yangchow fried rice (p.113), or stir-fried ten varieties (p.101).

2 lb (900 g) belly pork
1–2 spring onions
2–3 pieces fresh ginger root
1 teaspoon salt
1 teaspoon Five Spice powder
3 tablespoons Chinese rice wine or sherry
3 tablespoons crystallized (or rock) sugar
5 tablespoons soy sauce (2 of dark and 3 of light)
lettuce or cabbage leaves for garnish

If you bought the pork in one or two big pieces, cut it into large chunks about 6 in×3 in (150 mm×75 mm). Place it in a large saucepan with the spring onions, ginger root, salt, Five Spice powder, wine, sugar, soy sauce, and just enough cold water to cover. Bring it to a rolling boil, and keep the heat fairly high for about 2 hours, adding a little water now and again to keep it from drying out, but otherwise keeping the lid firmly closed so that the meat juices do not seep out.

To serve, remove the meat from the sauce, cut it into thin slices rather like rashers of bacon, and serve it on a bed of lettuce leaves or cooked cabbage. The sauce can be stored and re-used for cooking other meat or chicken, or the egg dish on p.56.

o Crystal-boiled pork

This is a famous recipe from Shanghai, traditionally served cold. Like the Cantonese white-cut chicken, it is very easy to make.

2–2½ lb (900–1.1 kg) leg of pork, boned but not skinned

For the sauce:
1–2 cloves garlic, crushed and finely chopped
2 spring onions, finely chopped
1 teaspoon finely chopped fresh ginger root
1 teaspoon sugar
3 tablespoons light soy sauce
1 tablespoon dark soy sauce
2 teaspoons sesame seed oil
1 teaspoon chilli sauce (optional)

As a starter or as part of a buffet-style meal, this dish will serve at least 10–12 people; so if you are cooking for a smaller number of people, then just serve the appropriate amount (remember to reduce the quantities for the sauce accordingly). The unused pork, wrapped so it is airtight, will keep in the refrigerator for 4–5 days. For best flavour and to preserve the moist texture, do not cut the meat until just before required. Besides being served cold either on its own or as a part of an assorted hors d'oeuvre, any leftovers can be used for a number of recipes which call for ready-cooked meat, such as twice-cooked pork (p.126).

Place the pork, tied together in one piece with lengths of string, in a large pot; add cold water to cover, and bring it to a rolling boil. Skim off the scum and simmer gently under cover for about 1 hour, turning it over once or twice during cooking. Then take it off the heat and let the pork stay in the liquid for at least 3–4 hours before removing it to cool, under cover with the skin side up, for a further 4–6 hours.

Just before serving, cut off the skin and any excess fat, leaving only a very thin layer of fat on top like a ham joint. Then cut the meat into small thin slices across the grain – you will find it is much easier to do this if you chill the meat in the refrigerator (but not in the freezer) for a few hours to harden it slightly. Put any uneven bits and pieces in the centre of a plate, arrange the well-cut slices in two neat rows, one on each side of the pile, then carefully arrange a third row on top of the pile so that it resembles an arched bridge.

Either pour the sauce evenly all over the pork and serve, or mix the sauce in little saucers as a dip.

o 'Agitated' kidney flowers

A simple-to-prepare dish from Peking which, when served side by side with 'agitated' prawns (p.63), gives an interesting contrast in texture and colour as well as flavour.

Readers must forgive me for introducing this rather unusual cooking method called 'agitating'. The Chinese term is *giang*, which is hard to define. It can be loosely translated as 'to excite', and involves marinating the parboiled or deep-fried ingredients with highly flavoured seasonings such as vinegar, wine and ginger root. But I thought if you served 'excited kidneys' to your guests they might get the wrong idea, so I have used the term 'agitated' instead.

— 1 pair pork kidneys, about ½ lb (225 g)

2–3 slices fresh ginger root, peeled and thinly shredded
½ teaspoon salt
2 tablespoons Chinese rice wine or dry sherry
1 teaspoon sesame seed oil

The colour of pork kidneys should be bright reddish brown; do not buy any that have turned dark purple or that do not smell fresh. First peel off the thin white skin covering the kidneys if the butcher has not already done so, then split them in half lengthways and discard the fat and the white, tough parts in the middle. Score the surface of the kidneys diagonally in a criss-cross pattern and then cut them into thin slices so that when cooked they will open up and resemble ears of corn – hence 'kidney flowers'.

Parboil the kidneys in a pan of boiling water over high heat. Do not overcook: as soon as the water starts to reboil, quickly remove the kidneys and drain, then run cold water over them for a few seconds to prevent the kidneys getting too tough. Drain well and place them on a serving dish.

Now place the thinly shredded ginger root on the kidneys, then sprinkle the salt evenly all over the top, followed by the wine. Leave to marinate for a while, say 10–15 minutes. Add the sesame seed oil, mix and toss just before serving.

o Braised tripe

In the West, tripe (usually the stomach of ox, but the stomachs of sheep and pigs are sometimes used) is always sold thoroughly cleaned and treated, i.e. 'dressed': which means a lot of time saving both in preparation and cooking for you at home.

1½ lb (680 g) tripe
2 tablespoons oil
2 slices fresh ginger root
2 spring onions
1 teaspoon Five Spice powder
3 tablespoons Chinese rice wine or sherry

4 tablespoons soy sauce
1 tablespoon sugar
1 pint (600 ml) good stock or sauce from soy-braised chicken etc.
finely chopped spring onions to garnish

If the tripe has been frozen, make sure it is thoroughly defrosted, then just pat it dry with kitchen paper or towels. Heat the oil in a hot saucepan and lightly brown the tripe on all sides. Add all the ingredients and bring to the boil. (If you have any sauce left from soy-braised chicken (p.36) or fragrant pork (p.57), it can be used instead of or in addition to the stock.)

Reduce the heat and simmer gently under cover for about 1 hour, then turn off the heat and leave the tripe to cool in the sauce for 3–4 hours before removing it. The sauce should be strained and can be re-used again and again; it will keep for many weeks if stored in the refrigerator in an airtight container.

Cut the tripe into small, neat slices for serving. Any leftovers should be wrapped airtight and stored in the refrigerator. Left-overs can even be served hot if re-heated or cooked with other ingredients.

○ 'Smoked' fish

The interesting thing about this dish is that the fish is not smoked. It acquires a smoky taste from being first marinated in soy sauce and wine, then deep-fried in hot oil, and finally marinated in the specially prepared sauce.

1 lb (450 g) cod steaks or cutlets (or any other firm white fish)
2–3 tablespoons soy sauce
2–3 tablespoons Chinese rice wine or sherry
2 spring onions, finely chopped
2–3 slices fresh ginger root, peeled and finely chopped
2 tablespoons brown sugar
1 teaspoon Five Spice powder
½ pt (280 ml) stock or water
about 1 pt (600 ml) oil for deep-frying

Never use fish that has been frozen. Chilled fish should be patted dry with kitchen paper or towels and should not be cut into small pieces or skinned.

Marinate the fish with soy sauce and wine for at least 30 minutes, turning them over once or twice. Remove the pieces and add to the marinade the finely chopped spring onions, ginger root, sugar, Five Spice powder and stock or water. Bring this mixture to the boil in a small saucepan, then reduce the heat and simmer gently for 10 minutes or so. Strain through a fine sieve and keep the sauce.

Heat up the oil in a deep-fryer or wok until very hot (you will see a haze forming above the surface of the oil), drop in the fish steaks or cutlets one at a time and fry for about 5 minutes or until they are crisp and golden. Then pick them out with chopsticks or a perforated spoon and immerse them in the sauce to cool for 15–20 minutes before laying them out side by side on a dish to dry.

The remainder of the sauce can be stored in the refrigerator for up to 4–5 days and used again.

o Phoenix-tail prawns

These prawns are deep-fried in their shells with the tails still attached, which is decorative and makes them easy to handle. For best results, use raw giant prawns sometimes called king prawns. They are usually sold headless and are grey in colour, turning bright pink only when they are cooked.

— 1 lb (450 g) king prawns in their shells
1 tablespoon light soy sauce
½ teaspoon Sichuan pepper
3 tablespoons Chinese rice wine or sherry
2 teaspoons cornflour
2 eggs, lightly beaten
4 tablespoons breadcrumbs
oil for deep-frying (about 1 pt/600 ml)

For serving:
2–3 spring onions, thinly shredded
lettuce leaves

Thoroughly defrost the prawns, then wash and dry them with kitchen paper or towel. Remove the legs by pulling them off with your fingers, but keep the body shells and tails on. Using a sharp knife, carefully slit along the underbelly – the inner curve where you have just removed the soft legs – cutting about ¾ of the way through the flesh. Remove the vein without cutting through the back shell. Spread the prawn out with the flesh side down, then gently tap once or twice with the flat side of the cleaver or knife to flatten the back a little so that the prawn spreads to a 'fan' or 'butterfly'.

When you have prepared all the prawns, marinate them with soy sauce, pepper, wine and cornflour – any additional seasonings, such as garlic salt, paprika, mild curry powder or barbecue seasoning, will only enhance the flavour.

Heat the oil until very hot, then turn the heat off to let the oil cool down a little. Meanwhile, lightly beat the eggs in a bowl and spread the breadcrumbs out on a flat plate.

One by one, pick up a prawn by the tail, dip it in the beaten egg then roll it in the breadcrumbs before lowering it into the oil. (You can in fact do two at a time if you use both hands.) After a while, turn the heat up to high again and cook the prawns in batches until golden brown, then remove with a perforated spoon and drain.

To serve, arrange the prawns neatly on a bed of lettuce leaves, and garnish with thinly shredded spring onions, either raw or soaked for about 30 seconds in the hot oil in which you have just cooked the prawns.

o 'Agitated' prawns

This dish would go well with 'agitated' kidney flowers (see the recipe on p.59, where the name 'agitated' is also explained).

½ lb (225 g) uncooked prawns
½ teaspoon salt
2 tablespoons Chinese rice wine or dry sherry
a few thin slices fresh ginger root, peeled
2 teaspoons sesame seed oil

If the prawns are frozen, make sure they are thoroughly thawed. Wash, shell and de-vein them, pat dry with kitchen paper or towel, then cut each prawn in half lengthways.

Bring about 2 pints (1 litre) of water to the boil in a saucepan, then add the prawns, stir and, as soon as they turn white, quickly scoop them out with a strainer and plunge them into a bowl of cold water for a few seconds. Drain well before placing them on a small serving dish.

Sprinkle the salt and wine evenly over the prawns, let it stand for a few minutes, then garnish with thinly shredded ginger root and sesame seed oil. Mix and toss just before serving.

IV

Chicken – Variations on a Theme

Braised chicken with green peppers
Diced chicken breast with celery
Diced chicken with green peppers
Diced chicken and lychees
Chicken balls and mushrooms
Chicken slices and bamboo shoots
Diced chicken in hot bean sauce
Hot chillis and diced chicken
Diced chicken and pork
Diced chicken with sweet bean sauce
Chicken wings assembly
Sliced chicken with ham and broccoli
Fu-yung (Lotus-white) chicken
Long-simmered whole chicken

See also:
Cold sliced chicken (p.26)
Soy-braised chicken (p.36)

For those of you who have had experience of eating Chinese food, whether in a restaurant or at a friend's home, probably the first thing you noticed was that very few Chinese dishes consist of only a single ingredient. In the earlier chapters I stressed the importance of harmony in Chinese cooking. This is achieved by a harmonious balance of various ingredients to attain a perfect blending and contrast between aroma, colour, flavour and texture.

To start with, you first choose your main ingredient (fish, chicken or meat), then decide which type or types of vegetable will go best with it, bearing in mind the differences of colour and texture and so on. For instance, if the main ingredient is chicken, which is pale white in colour and tender and delicate in texture, then one would choose something soft, like mushrooms, or crisp, like celery, or both, as the subsidiary ingredient, to give the dish a sort of harmonized texture. As an alternative, one might choose something more colourful, such as green and/or red peppers (crisp), and something crunchy, like nuts.

By combining different supplementary ingredients with the main one, you can produce an almost endless variety of dishes to astonish your family and friends. You will find this method of cooking is very economical, too, since as a rule each dish requires no more than ½ lb (225 g) each of meat and vegetables and two such dishes should be ample for three or four people for an everyday meal. A few years ago we used to stay with friends in the South of France for summer holidays. We were all appalled by the high food prices there, particularly of meat (this was in the days before Britain joined the Common Market). If we had had just a pork chop each – there were nine of us, counting the children – it would have cost a small fortune, whereas cooking in the Chinese way we spent far less and everybody, large and small, had a marvellous meal.

In China, chicken is treated as a greater delicacy than pork, and is regarded as especially nutritious. Besides being a festive dish, chicken is also eaten at everyday meals, partly because chickens are reared more or less domestically by every household and it is a relatively simple matter for a Chinese family to kill a chicken, prepare and cook it, either whole or in a number of different ways using different parts of the bird. This is especially true of people living in the countryside – which represents about 85 per cent of the Chinese population.

As you will have gathered, almost all Chinese chickens and ducks are free range, they have a firm flesh and are full of natural flavour. You may have also noticed the difference between a fresh farm bird and a battery-reared hen that has been frozen – they are as different as chalk and cheese: one is juicily succulent, the other is dry and tasteless. There is even a noticeable difference between the bird that has been chilled for days wrapped in plastic film in the supermarket and the fresh-killed poultry from a traditional family butcher.

Since we use only chopsticks at the table, a chicken or duck which has been cooked whole has to be cut into small bite-size pieces for serving. This is where a Chinese cleaver comes in very useful, but even without a cleaver, the task is made much easier if you follow the step-by-step instructions given below.

o Chopping up a whole chicken for serving

1. Detach the two wings at the joints, then cut each wing into two pieces at the joint. Discard the wing tips.
2. Detach the two thighs by cutting through the skin around the

joints with a sharp knife or the tip of the cleaver. Separate the legs (drumsticks) from the thighs through the joints, one at a time.

3. Lay the limbless chicken on its side and separate the breasts from the backbone section by cutting down through the soft bone from the tail to the neck.
4. Carve away the skin and meat from the backbone section, cut into small bite-size pieces and arrange them in a straight row in the centre of an oval serving platter.
5. Lay the chicken breasts on the skin and remove by hand the wishbone and the main breastbone. Turn the meat over so the skin side is now facing upward, cut the two breasts in half lengthwise, then chop each breast crosswise into small, neat pieces. Transfer the breast meat pieces, one half at a time, with the blade of the cleaver and arrange them on top of the backbone meat on the serving platter.
6. Chop the legs and thighs crosswise into small bite-size pieces and arrange them on each side of the breast halves. Arrange the two wings, one on each side, near the upper part of the breast meat so that the original shape of the chicken is now approximated.

Chicken breasts and other parts, such as wings, thighs and drumsticks, can all be bought separately, either filleted or still with the skin and bone. But it is more economical to buy a whole chicken from your favourite supplier, and joint it yourself – that way not only can you ensure the best quality and freshness of the meat, but you can also use the discarded bits and pieces for stock-making.

o Braised chicken with green peppers

A favourite practice of ours is to turn one chicken into two contrasting dishes. (This can also be done with meat: Lions' heads (p.37) and the pork and mushroom soup recipes (p.39) for example.)

1 tender roasting chicken (3 lb/1.4 kg or more)
flour for dusting
2–3 tablespoons oil
2 cloves garlic, crushed
1–2 slices ginger root, peeled and cut into small pieces
1 teaspoon salt
1 tablespoon sugar
2 tablespoons light soy sauce
3 tablespoons Chinese rice wine or sherry
½ lb (225 g) green peppers, cored and seeded

Lay the chicken on its side. Holding the top firmly with one hand, use a boning knife or the tip of a Chinese cleaver to cut lengthways along the curved breastbone with your other hand, slowly cutting the breast meat off the bones by following the side of the bone and the outside of the ribs. Repeat the same action on the other side and pull the meat off the bones and away from the skin, using the knife if necessary to free it. These two pieces of chicken breast you put aside for the next dish.

Now turn the breastless chicken so that it is breastbone down, preferably on a kitchen towel to prevent its slipping. With the boning knife, cut along the spine from top to tail without cutting through the bones. Probe with your fingers to locate the joint between the wing and the shoulder, then sever. Repeat the same action on the other side.

Next, separate the two 'oysters' from the carcass, and snap the joints between the thighs and the carcass. Continue to pull the meat all the way down to the tail bone, then detach it. Cut the remaining chicken into 8 pieces by separating the thighs and drumsticks, and the first and mid-portion of the wings. (The wing-tips and other bits and pieces, together with the carcass, are destined for the stock pot.)

Lightly dust the 8 chicken pieces with flour. (You should get 4–6 servings out of them if you are also serving the diced chicken breast dish; you can stretch them to serve 8–10 if you chop the 8 pieces into about 20 bite-size small chunks.)

Heat the oil in a pre-heated saucepan or large frying pan which has a lid, add the crushed garlic and ginger pieces to flavour the oil, then turn down the heat to moderate before adding the chicken pieces. Stir until they are lightly brown all over. Now add salt, sugar, soy sauce and wine. Continue stirring for a little while, then add a little stock or water – about 7 fl oz (200 ml) at most – increase the heat to high again to bring the liquid to the boil, then reduce the heat and simmer gently under cover for about 20–25 minutes. You have to be careful that the sauce does not run dry so that the pieces get stuck on the bottom of the pan: if you are using a deep saucepan, stir the pieces of chicken once or twice to make sure they are evenly cooked.

About 5 minutes before serving, stir in the green peppers cut into pieces roughly the size of a postage stamp, add a little more water or stock if necessary, then turn up the heat. Leave the lid off this time and let the contents bubble a while so that there is not too much liquid left.

o Diced chicken breast with celery

While the first chicken dish is being cooked, you can start to prepare this one, but do not cook it until the last minute, just before serving.

chicken breast meat (see previous recipe)
1 teaspoon salt
½ egg white, lightly beaten
2 teaspoons cornflour mixed with 1 tablespoon cold water
1 small head celery
1–2 spring onions
3–4 tablespoons oil
1 tablespoon light soy sauce
1 tablespoon Chinese rice wine or sherry

Separate the meat from the white tendon and membrane of the chicken breast, dice it into cubes the size of sugar lumps. Mix it with a pinch of the salt, then egg white and finally the cornflour and water solution – in that order, *not* all together – this is very important.

Cut the celery diagonally into small cubes roughly the same size as the chicken cubes. Cut the spring onions into small pieces, also diagonally.

To cook, warm the oil in a pre-heated wok or frying pan, stir-fry the chicken cubes over moderate heat for a short time or until it is half done, then scoop out with a perforated spoon. Next bring up the fire to heat the remaining oil (if there is not enough, add some more), throw in the spring onions first to flavour the oil, and immediately follow with the celery. Stir-fry for ½ minute or so with the remaining salt, then add the chicken and cook together for about another ½ minute. Now add the soy sauce and wine and continue stirring for about 1 minute (at the very most).

Serve hot. The chicken should be tender and the celery should be crisp and crunchy.

With boiled rice, you should easily be able to make at least six helpings out of these two dishes; or you can make two meals by serving them one at a time on two separate occasions.

Naturally you don't have to buy a whole chicken in order to make these two dishes. Most butchers and supermarkets will sell you chicken pieces already cut up, though their quality may not be top-grade. But if you are cooking for two or three people, you need only small quantities, otherwise the dish ceases to be economical.

Stir-fried diced chicken is one of the most popular dishes in China. The recipe I have just given you was passed on to me by my mother, who in turn learnt it from her mother, so you might say it is a truly traditional family recipe. Of course it goes without saying that you can easily substitute almost any kind of vegetable for the celery, according to the season and your taste. I have come across at least half a dozen variations on this dish, all of them highly recommended. You will find them all basically very similar, and the cooking methods are the same, but it is in the varying use of supplementary ingredients and condiments that the subtle differences lie. After you have tried some or all of them, you can then decide which is your favourite. Who knows, you might even make up your own variation, borrowing some ideas from these recipes, and that is the true spirit of Chinese cooking.

Diced chicken with green peppers

This is a Cantonese recipe. It is very colourful and delicious, but it calls for a few rather unusual ingredients which can be either omitted or substituted. If you have difficulty in finding dried mushrooms, use fresh ones, though the flavour will be different. You should have no difficulty in getting canned bamboo shoots from delicatessens or most supermarkets, otherwise substitute courgettes (if in season) or even young carrots.

½ lb chicken meat (boned and skinned)
1 tablespoon rice wine or sherry
1–2 slices ginger root, peeled and finely chopped
½ egg white, lightly beaten
2 teaspoons cornflour
4–5 dried mushrooms, soaked (or ¼ lb/100 g fresh mushrooms)
¼ lb (100 g) bamboo shoots
½ lb (225 g) green peppers, cored and seeded
1 clove garlic, crushed and finely chopped
1 spring onion, finely chopped
3–4 tablespoons oil
1½ teaspoons salt
1 teaspoon sugar

Dice the chicken as before, mix it with the wine and ginger root and add egg white and cornflour. Then dice the mushrooms, squeezed dry and with the stalks removed, and also dice the bamboo shoots and green peppers. Finely chop the garlic and spring onion.

To cook, warm up a little oil in a pre-heated wok or frying pan and stir-fry the chicken for a short while. Scoop it out with a perforated spoon, then heat up the rest of the oil, throw in the garlic and spring onion, followed by the green peppers, mushrooms and bamboo shoots, and stir for about ½ minute. Now add salt and sugar, and return the half-cooked chicken to the pan and stir-fry all together for about one minute. Serve hot.

You will notice that no soy sauce is used in this recipe. In the original edition of this book, I followed the Chinese instruction by advocating the use of a very small amount of monosodium glutamate. I did point out that the question of MSG is a controversial one. In the past, it was widely used in the run-of-the-mill Chinese restaurants both at home and abroad, very often to excess, with the result that a few people suffered actual physical discomfort. Let me stress the point that there were never a great number of people involved, otherwise they would have steered clear of Chinese restaurants when eating out. If large numbers of people are affected by MSG, how can one explain the recent and ever-increasing popularity of Chinese cooking in the West? There followed a worldwide scare that MSG was harmful to your health. Personally, I believe this fear is more based on ignorance than concrete evidence. I am sure you will agree that, like most pleasures in life, excess should be avoided, as in such everyday items as salt, sugar or alcohol.

In case you want to know what all the fuss is about, I would just like to say that monosodium glutamate is a chemical compound sometimes known as *veh t'sin* or 'taste powder' because it is supposed to enhance the natural flavour of ingredients that are past their prime. It should be used very discreetly, otherwise all dishes will have a uniform taste. A good cook in China regards it as cheating to resort to the use of this artificial seasoning. I remember as a child in China I was told that because 'taste powder' was invented in Japan it was a Japanese plot to make the entire Chinese male population sterile. So now you have been warned!

Diced chicken and lychees

Talking of sterility reminded me of another recipe which is supposed to have the opposite effect – it is traditionally given to a young person on reaching puberty as an extra boost to his or her reproductive system. It had rather a strange taste as I remember it, but then the Chinese believe all good medicine should taste nasty, so you might decide to risk it. Anyway, I am only including it here for your curiosity.

½ lb (225 g) chicken meat
1 teaspoon salt
1 tablespoon cornflour
2 slices ginger root, peeled and finely chopped
1 spring onion, finely chopped
1 clove garlic, crushed and finely chopped
10 oz (280 g) lychees
3–4 tablespoons oil
2 tablespoons rice wine or sherry
salt and pepper to taste

Logically enough, you are only supposed to use the meat of a young cock – capon is definitely out. Dice it as for previous recipes and mix with a pinch of salt and a little cornflour. Finely chop the ginger root, spring onion and garlic. Now for the lychees. Strictly speaking you should use fresh longans or 'dragons' eyes', a smaller variety of lychees. Their flesh is firmer and therefore tastier, but unfortunately they are rather hard to come by, even canned ones, and lychees are adequate substitutes. If you can get fresh ones in season so much the better. Just peel off the shells and extract the stones. Canned lychees are very easy to obtain; you should drain off the syrup and rinse them in cold water before using them.

First stir-fry the diced chicken in a little warm oil until done – but don't overcook. Then heat up more oil, add the ginger root, spring onion and garlic. Stir for a few seconds, then add the cooked chicken and lychees together with salt, wine, and cornflour mixed with a little water. Blend them well, adjust seasonings, and serve as soon as the liquid starts to thicken.

Well, good breeding!

o Chicken balls and mushrooms

Do not be deceived by the name of this dish into thinking that we are using a certain part of the chicken's anatomy: the balls are in fact chicken meat cut into small pieces so that when they are cooked, they will look like little round balls. (The same applies to meat balls and prawn balls). This is an orthodox recipe from Canton, and is very simple.

½ lb (225 g) chicken breast meat
1 teaspoon salt
2 teaspoons cornflour
½ lb (225 g) button mushrooms
2–3 spring onions, finely chopped (keep the white and green parts separate)
1 pt (600 ml) oil
1 tablespoon light soy sauce

Use small white button mushrooms, leaving them whole. Cut the chicken into pieces roughly the same size as the mushrooms, and mix in a little salt and about half of the cornflour blended with cold water.

Heat the oil in a wok or deep-fryer until hot, then turn off the heat and let the oil cool down a little before adding the chicken. Stir to separate the pieces, and, as soon as their colour changes from pale pink to white, quickly scoop them out with a perforated spoon and drain.

Pour off all but 2 tablespoons oil, and turn the heat to high again. Wait for the oil to smoke before adding the white part of the spring onions together with the mushrooms. Stir a few times, then add the salt and chicken. Continue stirring for about 1 minute. Finally, add soy sauce, the green part of the spring onions, and the remaining cornflour blended with a little water.

Stir for a few times more. Serve as soon as the liquid starts to thicken.

Chicken slices and bamboo shoots

This recipe originated in Shanghai but it is very popular throughout China. It is a sort of standard dish served as a starter to whet your appetite for bigger things to follow and is regarded as an ideal accompaniment to wine drinking. The chicken can be, and often is, substituted by any other kind of meat such as pork, beef or liver.

½ lb (225 g) chicken meat
1 teaspoon salt
½ egg white, lightly beaten
1 teaspoon cornflour mixed with a little cold water
¼ lb (100 g) bamboo shoots
1 oz (25 g) Wooden Ears (black fungus)
2–3 spring onions, cut into short lengths
2 slices ginger root, peeled and cut into small bits
3–4 tablespoons oil
1 teaspoon sugar
1 tablespoon light soy sauce
2 tablespoons rice wine or sherry
a few drops sesame seed oil

Cut the chicken meat into small slices, then mix them with a pinch of salt, the egg white and the cornflour. Drain and slice the bamboo shoots. Soak the Wooden Ears in water (discard the hard bits at the root) and slice them too. First stir-fry the chicken in a little warm oil for about ½ minute, and scoop it out with a perforated spoon. Now heat up more oil until hot, add the spring onions and ginger root first to flavour the oil, then stir-fry the bamboo shoots and Wooden Ears for about ½ minute. Now add salt, sugar, soy sauce and wine together with about 2 table-spoons stock or water. Continue stirring, and when the sauce is bubbling, return the chicken to the pan, stir for a few times more, then add sesame seed oil. Blend everything well and serve immediately.

(It makes my mouth water just to think about this dish!)

o Diced chicken in hot bean sauce

We are now in Sichuan, famous for its richly flavoured and piquant dishes. The chilli bean paste called for in this recipe can be substituted by crushed yellow bean paste mixed with chilli sauce.

½ lb (225 g) chicken meat
1 teaspoon salt
½ egg white, lightly beaten
1 teaspoon cornflour blended with a little cold water
½ lb (225 g) bamboo shoots
1–2 slices ginger root, peeled and finely chopped
2–3 spring onions, finely chopped
3–4 tablespoons oil
1 teaspoon sugar
1 tablespoon soy sauce
2 tablespoons rice wine or sherry
1 tablespoon chilli bean paste

The chicken meat can be either breast or leg, or a mixture of both. Dice it into small cubes, mix with a pinch of salt, egg white and cornflour.

Dice the bamboo shoots, finely chop the ginger root and spring onions. Have all the seasonings and sauce at hand.

First stir-fry the chicken and bamboo shoots in warm oil for about 1 minute, then scoop them out with a perforated spoon. Heat up the oil again, stir-fry the spring onions and ginger root and add the chicken and bamboo shoots together with all the seasonings and sauce. Stir to make sure everything is well blended before serving. It should taste tender with a touch of hotness, an ideal starter.

o Hot chillis and diced chicken

Also known as 'Kung Bo' or 'Gong Bao' chicken, this is another famous Sichuan dish that has become popular throughout the world. It is reputed to have been one of Chairman Mao's favourites, because he was a native of Hunan, a neighbouring province, also known for its hot, peppery food.

½ lb (225 g) chicken meat
¼ teaspoon salt
½ egg white, lightly beaten
2 teaspoons cornflour blended with 1 tablespoon cold water
2 oz (50 g) fresh chilli, or 4 oz (100 g) green peppers with
  1 tablespoon chilli sauce
2 oz (50 g) cashew nuts (or walnuts, almonds, or peanuts)
3–4 tablespoons oil
2 slices peeled ginger root, finely chopped
2 spring onions, finely chopped
1 teaspoon sugar
1 tablespoon soy sauce
2 tablespoons rice wine or sherry
1 tablespoon crushed yellow bean paste

If you cannot get fresh chillis, then use green peppers with a little chilli sauce; the general effect will be the same even though the flavour is slightly different.

After dicing the chicken into small cubes, mix them with salt, egg white and cornflour. Cut the chilli or green pepper into pieces the same size as the chicken cubes.

Stir-fry the chicken in a little warm oil for about ½ minute, then scoop out with a perforated spoon. Heat up more oil, stir-fry the finely chopped ginger root and spring onions together with chilli or green pepper and nuts, add sugar, soy sauce, wine and bean paste, then return the chicken to the pan. Stir constantly for about 1 minute, and serve as soon as everything is well blended.

o Diced chicken and pork

This is a Peking dish. The pork must be the tenderest fillet (called tenderloin in the USA); when cooked, its colour turns to a pale white, almost the same as chicken breast, but with a subtle difference in taste and texture.

½ lb (225 g) chicken breast meat
½ lb (225 g) pork fillet
½ teaspoon salt
1 egg white, lightly beaten
2 teaspoons cornflour blended with 1 tablespoon cold water
3 tablespoons oil

For the sauce:
3 cloves garlic, crushed and finely chopped
2–3 spring onion stalks, finely chopped
1 tablespoon crushed yellow bean paste
1 tablespoon Hoi Sin sauce
1 tablespoon rice wine or sherry
2 teaspoons cornflour blended with about 3 tablespoons water

Dice the chicken and pork into small cubes, then in separate bowls, mix them with salt, egg white and cornflour. In a third bowl, mix the sauce which is called 'yellow sauce', and should be of a rather thick consistency.

First stir-fry the diced chicken in a little warm oil for a very short while, and scoop it out with a perforated spoon when it is half done. Do the same with the pork. Then turn up the heat, but before the oil gets too hot, return both the chicken and pork to the pan, followed by the 'yellow sauce'. Stir, and when the meats are well coated by the sauce with hardly any liquid left in the pan, the dish is ready for serving.

o Diced chicken with sweet bean sauce

This is another Peking dish, much simpler, and therefore easier to prepare than the previous one.

½ lb (225 g) chicken breast meat
½ egg white, lightly beaten
1 teaspoon cornflour blended with a little cold water
3 tablespoons oil
1 tablespoon crushed yellow bean paste
2 teaspoons sugar
1 tablespoon rice wine or sherry
1 teaspoon sesame seed oil

Dice the chicken breast into small cubes, mix in the egg white and cornflour, then stir-fry in warm oil until half-done. Scoop out with a perforated spoon, add the yellow bean paste, stir, then add sugar and wine and blend them well. Now add the sesame seed oil and continue stirring until smooth. Quickly put in the half-cooked chicken, and stir to blend with the sauce. When the colour turns golden, then it is ready. It should taste tender with a suggestion of sweetness, and the colour should be bright and glittering golden.

o Chicken wings assembly

'Assembly' is a translation of the Chinese word *hui*, which refers to food recooked in gravy thickened with cornflour. Most supermarkets sell chicken wings and legs separately. They are usually sold 4–6 to a pack, and are very good value.

12 chicken wings
1 teaspoon sugar
1 tablespoon light soy sauce
1 tablespoon dark soy sauce
2 tablespoons rice wine or sherry
1 teaspoon cornflour
1 clove garlic, crushed
2–3 spring onions, cut into short lengths
3 tablespoons oil
1 tablespoon crushed yellow bean paste
about 4 fl oz (125 ml) stock or water

Trim off and discard the tip of the wings (they can be used for making stock), and cut the remains of the wings into two pieces by breaking the joint. Mix them with sugar, soy sauce, wine and cornflour, and marinate for at least 25–30 minutes, stirring once or twice.

Cut the spring onions and crush the garlic.

Heat the oil in a pre-heated wok or large frying pan that has a fitting lid. When the oil is hot, take the chicken wings out of the marinade and lightly brown them, then scoop out with a perforated spoon. Now fry the garlic and spring onions followed by crushed yellow bean paste, add a little stock or water and stir to make a smooth gravy. Then add the chicken wings together with the marinade and more stock or water, stir and bring to the boil, then place a lid tightly over the pan and keep the heat fairly high. Listen carefully for the sizzling noise to make sure it is not burning. After a few minutes add a little more stock or water and stir gently to make sure that the chicken pieces are not stuck to the bottom of the pan. Then replace the lid and cook for further 5–10 minutes, until almost all the sauce is absorbed – then the dish is ready to serve.

The following recipes are for special occasions. They can be served on their own if there are only a few of you, or they can form part of a feast or banquet (see Chapter IX).

o Sliced chicken with ham and broccoli

This is a famous Cantonese dish which is both itself colourful and has a rather colourful name: 'golden flower and jade tree chicken'. 'Golden flower' (Jinhua) is a county in Southeast China which produces about the best ham in the world. (Writing in *The Compleat Imbiber* No. 11, Henri Gault, one of the two authors of the Juillard gastronomic guides, remarked that after tasting Chinese ham the best Parma ham seemed to taste like cardboard!) 'Jade' refers to the colour of the chicken and 'tree', of course, to the broccoli.

1 roasting chicken (3–3½ lb/1.4–1.6 kg)
2 spring onions
2–3 slices ginger root, unpeeled
1 tablespoon salt
1 lb (450 g) broccoli (or asparagus or green cabbage)
3 tablespoons oil
1 teaspoon sugar
½lb (225g) cooked ham (or bacon steak)
2 teaspoons cornflour

Place the chicken in a large pan and cover it with cold water, add the spring onions, ginger root and about 2 teaspoons salt. Bring it to the boil, then reduce heat and simmer gently for 5 minutes under a tightly fitting lid. Turn off the heat and let the chicken cook itself in the hot water for at least 3–4 hours – you must not open the lid, as this would let out the residual heat – in fact it is best to place a heavy weight on top of the pan to make sure that no heat escapes.

Just before serving, take the chicken out of the pan and carefully remove the meat from the bones but keep the skin on. Then slice both the chicken meat and ham into pieces the size of a matchbox and arrange them in alternating overlapped layers on a large plate.

Meanwhile wash the broccoli in cold water and stir-fry it in hot oil with 1 teaspoon each of salt and sugar, adding a little chicken stock if required. When it is done, arrange it around the edge of the plate.

Heat up a small amount of chicken stock with cornflour, stir until smooth, then pour it over the chicken and ham so that it forms a thin coat of transparent jelly resembling jade.

o Fu-yung (Lotus-white) chicken

This is a rather complicated but not too difficult recipe. What you need here is patience; the result is most satisfying and delicious.

In most Chinese restaurants, a 'fu-yung' dish usually means omelette or scrambled eggs, but strictly speaking, 'lotus-white' should be creamy-textured egg whites that have been lightly deep-fried, which prompted a certain imaginative cook to call this dish 'deep-fried milk'!

¼ lb (100 g) chicken breast meat
1 tablespoon cornflour mixed with 2 tablespoons cold water
5 egg whites, lightly beaten
1 teaspoon salt
1 fl oz (25 ml) milk or good stock
1 pt (600 ml) oil
4 fl oz (125 ml) good stock
1 tablespoon rice wine or sherry
1 oz (25 g) green peas
1 oz (25 g) cooked ham, finely chopped
a few drops of sesame seed oil

The best parts of the breast to use for this recipe are the two strips just along the breastbone. First pound the meat for about five minutes using the blunt edge of the cleaver and adding a little cold water now and again. Then chop the meat with the sharp edge of the blade for a further 5–10 minutes or until the meat has a creamy texture.

Make a smooth batter with the cornflour and water, add the chicken meat, egg whites, milk and a pinch of salt.

Heat up a wok or deep-fryer over high heat before putting in the oil (this is very important, otherwise the meat will stick to the bottom during frying). When the oil is really hot, turn off the heat to let it cool down to moderate before pouring in the fu-yung spoon by spoon. When the entire lot has been added to the oil, turn up the heat to moderate and stir oil up from the bottom of pan to help the fu-yung rise – but make sure not to touch them or they will scatter. As soon as they are set, scoop out with a perforated spoon and drain, then place them in a serving dish.

Heat up the remaining stock, add salt, wine and peas, thicken with a little more cornflour and water mixture, then pour over the fu-yung. Sprinkle the finely chopped ham and sesame seed oil as garnish and serve hot.

Should you wonder what on earth can you do with the egg yolks, after using only the egg whites for all these poultry and seafood dishes, the answer is quite simple: they can be added to scrambled eggs or omelette (have you noticed how much brighter is the colour of eggs used for fried rice in Chinese restaurants?), or indeed you can use them for cake-making etc. As a last resort, you can always give them to your pets (our cat loves egg yolk)! Nothing is ever wasted in Chinese cooking, least of all good food, which is too precious to throw away.

Long-simmered whole chicken

This is really a soup dish, but the chicken is served whole with the broth.

'Long-simmering' (the Chinese term is *dun*) is a very simple method of cooking. You first plunge the ingredient into boiling water for 2–3 minutes, then rinse it in cold water before the long-simmering starts. The purpose of this rapid boiling and rinsing process is to seal in the juice as well as to get rid of the impurities of the poultry or meat. During the long-simmering, very few supplementary ingredients are used – or none at all, as in this recipe – and the seasoning, which again is usually very simple, is not added until just before the completion of cooking, so that you end up with a dish of 'purity'. Because of this pure and simple method of cooking, long-simmered food is very good for invalids, or if served at a banquet ideal as a 'bridge-gap' after several richly prepared dishes and before some more, even richer, food to come.

1 young chicken (about 3 lb/1.4 kg)
2 spring onions, trimmed
2–3 slices ginger root, peeled

2–3 tablespoons rice wine, sherry or brandy
plenty of boiling water
salt and pepper to taste

Wash and clean the chicken well before plunging it into a large pot of boiling water. Let it boil rapidly for 2–3 minutes, then take out the bird and rinse it thoroughly under the cold tap.

Now place the chicken in a saucepan or casserole that has a tightly fitting lid, add about 3½ pt (2 litres) boiling water together with spring onions, ginger root and wine or brandy. Bring to the boil, use a strainer to remove the impurities that float to the surface, then reduce the heat and simmer gently under cover for 1½–2 hours, turning the chicken over once or twice and at the same time removing any impurities.

Adjust seasonings just before serving. The chicken should be so tender that one can easily tear it into shreds by using one's chopsticks or the soup spoon.

Any leftovers can be warmed up and served again. Why not strain the liquid and use it as stock or as a basis for soup-making – vegetables such as cabbage, carrots or turnips (also known as Chinese radish or mouli) can be added to make it into a delicious and nourishing soup. You can pull the chicken meat off the bones and serve it cold with a dip sauce. Since the meat served without soup would taste quite bland, you will need a fairly piquant sauce to make it more palatable. Try one made of finely chopped garlic, ginger root and spring onions with soy sauce and chilli sauce.

V

More Vegetables than Meat

Stir-fried green cabbage
Braised Chinese cabbage
Hot and sour cabbage
Fried spinach (also spinach with eggs)
Fried lettuce
Braised aubergines
Bean curd with mushrooms
Vegetarian eight precious jewels
Stir-fried four treasures
Eggs with tomatoes
Fried rice
Stir-fried ten varieties
 (i) with giblets
 (ii) with meats
Shredded pork with bean sprouts
Pork and french beans
Pork and cauliflower
Shredded pork with Sichuan preserved vegetable
Meat slices with spring onions
Shredded pork with green peppers
Stuffed green peppers
Pork laurel (mu-shu pork)
Pork laurel Shandong style
Thin pancakes
Yangchow fried rice
Fried noodles or chow mein
Noodles in soup
Vegetarian noodles in soup

See also:
Stir-fried pork and seasonal greens (p.29)
Fried beef and tomatoes (p.40)
Bean curd *à la maison* (p.125)
Sweet and sour cucumber (p.55)
Pickled radishes (p.56)
Braised eggs (p.56)

There are innumerable varieties of cabbage grown throughout China, and since the season lasts all the year round, cabbage forms part of the everyday diet. It is rich in vitamin C and minerals and has a delicious crunchy texture when cooked the Chinese way. Many people may not realize that the *Brassica* family includes not just the green, white and red cabbages, but also brussels sprouts, cauliflower, broccoli, mustard green, kale and so on. (You will find a wok particularly useful for cooking large-leaved vegetables which are hard to fit into an ordinary frying pan.)

o Stir-fried green cabbage

Most people who are put off by the strong smell of boiled cabbage often encountered in restaurants or canteens (not to mention by early memories of school dinners) will be pleasantly surprised to find that if prepared and cooked in the Chinese way, the ordinary cabbage has a special flavour and the crunchy texture is quite different from that of the usual mushy bits, not to mention the fresh, natural colour that has been retained by this quick stir-frying method.

In Britain, the cabbage season lasts almost all year round too: from April to the end of summer there are the oval-shaped spring cabbage of brilliant green; from September to February the winter cabbage which is round with a firm heart. Between these two seasons there are enough other varieties, some early and some late, to ensure a continual supply.

1 small green cabbage (about 1 lb/450 g)
1 spring onion
3 tablespoons oil
a few Sichuan peppercorns (optional)
1 teaspoon salt
2 teaspoons light soy sauce

Choose a cabbage that is young and fresh and discard any tough outer leaves. Wash it under the cold tap before cutting it into thin strips as for sauerkraut or coleslaw. Finely chop the spring onion.

Heat up a wok or frying pan, pour in the oil and swirl it in the wok or pan to cover most of the area. When the oil is hot, throw in the peppercorns, if using, then after a few seconds scoop them out before they are burnt and discard. Now throw in the finely chopped spring onion, followed almost immediately by the cabbage, stirring constantly for about 1 minute. Add salt and soy sauce, stir a few more times, and it is done. Do not overcook, otherwise the cabbage will lose its crispness as well as a great deal of its vitamin content, but keep the heat as high as you possibly can all the time.

o Braised Chinese cabbage

Chinese cabbage is now widely available both in America and Europe and is sometimes known as Chinese leaves or *Bok-choy*. One species has light green leaves with a long white stem and it forms a fairly tight and compact head on maturity. Another species has a shorter and fatter head with curlier, pale yellow leaves. One of the advantages of Chinese cabbage is that it will keep fresh for a long time and its texture will retain its crunchiness even after lengthy cooking – that's why it is so good for the lions' heads dish (p. 37).

1 lb (450 g) Chinese cabbage
1 spring onion
3 tablespoons oil
1 teaspoon salt

Wash the cabbage in cold water and discard any tough, tired or dry-looking outer leaves, then slice it into small pieces about the size of a matchbox. Finely chop the spring onion.

Place a wok or large frying pan over high heat, and when it is hot pour in the oil and swirl it about. When it starts to smoke, throw in the spring onion. Don't let it go brown, but throw in the cabbage and stir until all the pieces are covered with oil. Add salt and continue stirring; there should be enough natural juice to keep it from burning for at least 2 minutes or so. Again, do not overcook, and never cover the pan with a lid while cooking.

o Hot and sour cabbage

This was originally a Sichuan dish but it is now very popular throughout China. Naturally, there are several versions as people from different regions have adapted it to their taste. This recipe is supposed to be the authentic one, as it was given to my mother by one of her friends who is a native of Sichuan.

1½ lb (680 g) green or white cabbage
a few dried red chillis
about 10–12 Sichuan peppercorns
3–4 tablespoons oil
1½ teaspoons salt

For the sauce:
2 tablespoons soy sauce
2 tablespoons vinegar
1½ tablespoons sugar
1 teaspoon sesame seed oil

Choose a round, pale green cabbage with a firm heart, as fresh as possible; the white Dutch variety is a good substitute, but never use loose-leafed spring greens. Wash it in cold water, and tear the leaves by hand into small pieces the size of a matchbox. Cut the red chillis into small bits (discard the seeds if you don't like it hot!), mix the sauce in a bowl and have it handy.

First heat the wok or pan, add the oil and wait for it to smoke before throwing in the peppercorns and chillis to flavour the oil. Before they are burnt quickly add the cabbage, stir until it starts to go limp – this will take about 1 minute – then add salt and continue stirring for another ½ minute or so. Then pour in the sauce and stir for a short while to allow the sauce to mix in well. The cabbage is most delicious either hot or cold.

o Fried spinach

Spinach is known as 'Persian cabbage' in China. This dark green vegetable is full of iron and therefore highly regarded for its nutritious value. The slight acid taste in your mouth when eating spinach (caused by potassium oxalate) can be somewhat reduced if you cook it in the following manner:

1 lb (450 g) fresh spinach
3 tablespoons oil
½ teaspoon salt
1 teaspoon sugar
1 tablespoon soy sauce
a few drops sesame seed oil

If you live near an Oriental food store you may be able to buy small fresh spinach done up in bundles (I have often come across them in Berwick Street market in London); these are much tastier than the large, pale green leaves. Wash the spinach well and shake off as much excess water as possible. If using the smaller type, keep the red root as it adds colour as well as flavour.

Heat up the wok or a large saucepan (no ordinary frying pan is big enough to hold all the raw spinach leaves), pour in at least 3 tablespoons of oil, swirl it around until it covers almost the entire pan, and heat it until it smokes. Stir-fry the spinach for about ½ minute, add salt and sugar, mixing well, followed by the soy sauce.

This is really the basic method of cooking all types of fresh vegetables in China. Of course the soy sauce can be omitted or be substituted by additional salt – some people would use monosodium glutamate, but I do not recommend it (see page 74).

Another popular way of serving spinach is to combine it with 2–3 scrambled eggs. Cook the eggs first, then add them to the spinach at the last stage. If you garnish this dish with a few slices of cooked ham, then it becomes really colourful as well as having an even better flavour.

Now if you serve this dish with some boiling water, it becomes an instant soup. In fact, you can apply this simple method of soup-making to many Chinese recipes – see my remarks under 'Pork and mushroom soup' (p.39).

Lettuce was first introduced into China from Europe in the sixth or seventh century, and was regarded as a luxury item at first. Nowadays it is widely grown throughout the country as an everyday vegetable.

There are two main varieties of lettuce: the round cabbage or romaine lettuce and the long cos lettuce – the crisp Webb's or iceberg lettuce were introduced into China only very recently. While lettuce is almost always used as a salad vegetable in the West, it is seldom eaten raw in China (see p.54). Perhaps you would like to try the following recipe for a change:

o Fried lettuce

The upright cos lettuce with its crisp leaves is best for this method of cooking (if you use round lettuce, then you will need more than one).

1 large cos lettuce
2–3 tablespoons oil
1 teaspoon salt, or 1 tablespoon oyster sauce

Wash the lettuce in cold water and discard the tough outer leaves. Tear the larger leaves into halves – never use a knife to cut them – and lightly shake off the excess water as you would when making salad.

Heat up a wok or large frying pan, pour in the oil and swirl it to cover most of the surface. When it starts to smoke, throw in the lettuce. This will make a loud noise, but don't be alarmed, just stir vigorously until all the leaves are coated with oil, just as you would when mixing and tossing salad with dressing. Then add the salt or oyster sauce and stir a few times more; by then the noise will be more subdued and the lettuce leaves will have become slightly limp. Quickly dish it out and serve.

Make sure you do not overcook the lettuce, otherwise it will lose its crispness and bright green colour.

o Braised aubergines

Although the aubergine (eggplant) originated in India, it is very common and popular in China. It is one of the very few vegetables that requires a longer cooking time than usual.

This is another recipe from Sichuan, where it is sometimes called *yu-xiang* (meaning 'fish-fragrant' or 'fish-flavoured') and sometimes translated as 'Aubergine with fish sauce'. But the interesting point is that no fish is used in the recipe – the sauce is normally used for cooking a fish dish, and hence the name.

1 lb (450 g) aubergines
1 pt (600 ml) oil
1–2 cloves garlic, crushed and finely chopped
2–3 spring onions, finely chopped
2 slices peeled ginger root, finely chopped
1 tablespoon soy sauce
1 tablespoon chilli bean paste (optional)

2 tablespoons rice wine or sherry
1 teaspoon sugar
2 teaspoons vinegar
a few drops sesame seed oil

Choose the long, purple variety of aubergine rather than the large, round kind, if possible. Wash in cold water and discard the stalks. Cut the aubergines into diamond-shaped chunks (always cut aubergines just before cooking, otherwise the white flesh will darken in colour, so you can cut them while waiting for the oil to get heated). Heat up the oil in a wok or deep-fryer until very hot, deep-fry the aubergine for about 3–4 minutes or until soft, scoop out with a perforated spoon or strainer, and drain.

Leave about 1 tablespoon of hot oil in the wok. Throw in the finely chopped garlic, spring onions (white parts only, keep the green parts for later) and ginger root to flavour the oil. Then add chilli bean paste (if using), soy sauce, wine, sugar, vinegar and a little stock or water. Stir to make into a smooth sauce and bring to the boil. Now add the aubergines and braise for about 1 minute, stirring constantly. Finally, add the green spring onions and sesame seed oil. Serve hot.

For the non-vegetarians, about ¼ lb (100 g) thinly shredded pork can be added to the 'fish sauce' to enhance the flavour. Add it just after the garlic, spring onions and ginger root, but before the rest of the seasonings.

o Bean curd with mushrooms

This is a purely vegetarian dish. It is very refreshing and therefore most welcome when served as the last course after a big and rich feast.

4–6 medium-sized dried mushrooms (or 4 oz/100 g fresh mushrooms)
4 cakes bean curd (see notes on bean curd, pp. 15 and 125)
3–4 tablespoons oil
1 teaspoon salt

1 teaspoon sugar
2 tablespoons rice wine or sherry
a few drops sesame seed oil
1 teaspoon cornflour
1 tablespoon light soy sauce

Soak the dried mushrooms in warm water for about 30 minutes, then squeeze them dry and discard the stalks – but keep the water for use as stock. Slice each square of bean curd into slices ¼ in (6 mm) thick, then cut each slice into 6 or 8 pieces.

First stir-fry the mushrooms in very hot oil for about ½ minute, then add about ¼ pt (140 ml) of the water in which the mushrooms have been soaking. Bring to the boil and add the bean curd with the salt, sugar and wine, stirring very gently to blend everything well. Let it bubble for about 1–1½ minutes, then add the sesame seed oil. (Make sure that there is enough liquid to prevent the bean curd sticking to the bottom of the wok.) Finally, mix the cornflour and soy sauce with a little water, pour it all over the bean curd so that it forms a clear, light glaze, and serve immediately.

o Vegetarian eight precious jewels

Unlike most of his counterparts in the Western world, the Chinese vegetarian strictly prohibits anything remotely connected with animals, including eggs and milk. He can eat only purely vegetable matter. In order to make their diet a little more exciting, the Buddhist monks and nuns and other vegetarians invented a special cuisine in China, including vegetarian dishes that simulate meat not only in texture and appearance but in flavour as well.

Naturally, these vegetarian foods require special skill and ingredients which are beyond the scope both of this book and of its author. However, I have adapted for Western kitchens one of their best-known dishes called 'eight precious jewels', using substitutes for some of the original ingredients which are rather hard to come by.

4–5 dried mushrooms (or 2 oz/50 g fresh mushrooms)
1 oz (25 g) dried bean curd skin
1 oz (25 g) dried Tiger Lily
1 oz (25 g) Wooden Ears (black fungus)
4 oz (100 g) bamboo shoots
2 oz (50 g) carrots
4 oz (100 g) Chinese cabbage (or celery)
4 oz (100 g) broccoli (or any green vegetable, such as french beans)
4 tablespoons oil
1 teaspoon salt
1 teaspoon sugar
1 tablespoon light soy sauce
1 teaspoon sesame seed oil

Soak all the dried vegetables separately in cold water overnight or in warm water for a few hours. Slice them into thin strips (except the Tiger Lily which is in small strips already). Slice the bamboo shoots, carrots, cabbage and broccoli.

Heat a wok or large pan. When it is hot put in about 2 tablespoons oil and wait till it smokes. Stir-fry all the dried vegetables together with the bamboo shoots, add a little water from the dried mushrooms, bring it to the boil for a few seconds, then dish it out. Now heat up more oil and stir-fry the carrots, cabbage (or celery) and broccoli (or greens) for about 1 minute, then add the partly-cooked dried vegetables with salt, sugar and soy sauce. Continue stirring for another minute. If the contents start to go dry, add a little more water to keep them from getting burnt. Add a few drops of sesame seed oil before serving.

This dish can be served cold if you prefer.

Stir-fried four treasures

This is a simplified variation of the 'Eight precious jewels' dish, rather like the mixed vegetables you get in a frozen packet, but with a difference.

5–6 dried mushrooms (or ¼ lb/100 g fresh mushrooms)
¼ lb (100 g) baby corn (also known as dwarf or young corn)
¼ lb (100 g) mange-touts peas
½ lb (225 g) carrots
3–4 tablespoons oil
1 teaspoon salt
1 teaspoon sugar
1 tablespoon rice wine or sherry (optional)
2 teaspoons light soy sauce

Soak the mushrooms in warm water for 30 minutes. Squeeze them dry, discard the stalks, and cut the mushrooms into thin slices. If fresh baby corns are not available, used canned ones. Leave them whole if tiny, otherwise cut each one into 3–4 small diamond-shaped pieces. Wash, top and tail the mange-touts. Thinly slice the carrots diagonally.

Heat the oil in a hot wok or large frying-pan. Stir-fry the carrots first, then the baby corn and mange-touts peas, and finally the mushrooms. After about 1 minute, add salt, sugar and wine. Continue stirring for another minute or so. Add the soy sauce and, if the vegetables dry out, a little water as well.

Serve as soon as all the liquid has evaporated.

o Eggs with tomatoes

The tomato is a native of South America and was not introduced into China until the end of the last century. Ideally you should use green, hard tomatoes for this recipe, but if you do not grow your own or are unable to find them on the market, then choose the most under-ripe and hard ones you can find.

½ lb (225 g) tomatoes
4 eggs
2 spring onions, finely chopped
1 teaspoon salt
4 tablespoons oil

Cut the tomatoes into slices. Beat the eggs with a pinch of salt and about a third of the finely chopped spring onions.

Heat about half the oil in a hot wok or frying pan and lightly scramble the eggs over a moderate heat until set but not too hard. Remove from pan. Heat the remaining oil over a high heat until smoking, and add the rest of the finely chopped spring onions and tomatoes. Add the salt and stir a few times, then add the scrambled eggs. Continue stirring for about ½ minute. Serve hot.

Other vegetables such as cucumber, green peppers or mange-touts peas can be substituted for the tomatoes.

Fried rice

4 cups cooked rice (for four people)
2–3 eggs
1–2 spring onions, finely chopped
some leftover cooked meat or vegetables (optional)
2–3 tablespoons oil
1 teaspoon salt

To use up any leftover cooked rice (allow 1 cup at least for each person), the best way is to stir-fry it in a little hot oil with scrambled eggs over a moderate heat. When all the grains are separated, add salt and finely chopped spring onions. If you happen to have any leftover cooked meat such as chicken, pork or ham, or vegetables such as peas, carrots or green pepper, dice them into small cubes the size of peas and add to the rice to improve not only its flavour and texture but also its appearance.

A recipe for a more elaborate version is to be found on p.113.

As I said earlier (p.8), stir-frying is by far the most frequently used cooking method in a Chinese home; practically all fresh vegetables are cooked in this way. After you have perfected your skill in this comparatively simple technique (heat and timing are the essentials), and aided by a little experimental spirit and imagination, you should be able to turn almost any ingredient into a successful dish without sticking strictly to the recipes, and thus you can produce more than '57 varieties' with ease.

For the time being we will stick to a few more homely dishes, mostly made by the quick stir-frying manner and using easily obtainable ingredients such as pork, beef, chicken, fish, eggs and any fresh vegetable that happens to be in season, as well as a selection from your store cupboard.

Any of these dishes should serve at least two people, or will stretch to four or five helpings if combined with another dish. Suppose you have prepared three different dishes for five people, and at the end you find that there was a small portion left of each. Don't think the leftovers will be wasted: if you mix them together and warm them up the next day you will have created your own 'chop suey', for that is precisely what a genuine chop suey should be – a hotch-potch of leftovers.

I wonder how many readers realize that the type of chop suey dishes one gets in a run-of-the-mill Chinese restaurant or cheap take-away in Europe and America is quite alien to the Chinese? There are several accounts of the origin of this most popular 'Chinese' dish outside China. According to my father, how it happened was like this: when the first ever Chinese restaurant was opened in San Francisco over a hundred years or so ago, not a single non-Chinese would dare to go in to try out this exotic eating place, and consequently there was quite a lot of ready-prepared food left over day after day. Finally, one courageous American – a drunken sailor, my father thought – staggered in and demanded the specialities of the house. The astonished cook, who was most probably having a nap out of boredom, quickly produced a mixture of whatever was at hand. Obviously the customer had never tasted anything like it in all his life, and wanted to know what he was eating. The equally surprised proprietor, who was a seaman himself, racked his brains and came out with the truth: he called the dish *zasui*, which literally translated is 'miscellaneous fragments', or to put it in simpler terms 'mixed bits'. Thus the world-famous chop suey was born.

If this story is true, that cook did not so much create an original dish as merely use his wits and do what any Chinese housewife would have done in the same situation when an unexpected guest called; but to actually serve a dish of leftovers in a restaurant was unheard of. In a sense, that cook unwittingly invented a new dish that was to become the symbol of Chinese restaurants abroad.

Stir-fried ten varieties (i) with giblets

In China, the Chinese have their own 'mixed bits', known as *zahui* or *shijin*, meaning 'assorted mixture' or 'ten varieties', though it may not always consist of ten different ingredients, nor should they all be leftovers. Indeed, all the ingredients are specially selected in order to achieve a perfect balance of texture, colour and flavour. The dish should have a distinct taste and should never be a jumbled mess like the type of chop suey one gets from most take-aways.

giblets from one or two chickens (or ducks)
3–4 Chinese dried mushrooms
1 small can bamboo shoots
6 oz (170 g) greens (mange-touts peas, broccoli, french beans etc)
2–3 spring onions
2 tablespoons soy sauce
2 tablespoons rice wine or sherry
2 teaspoons cornflour
3–4 tablespoons oil
1 teaspoon salt
a few drops sesame seed oil

In Western cooking terms, giblets means the head, neck, heart, pinions, feet, gizzard, kidneys and liver of poultry. These are normally used for making stock or, more often than not, discarded by people who do not know what to do with them. This is a pity because they not only have a high nutritive value but can also be made into excellent dishes. In China giblets are regarded as a delicacy.

For our dish, we only need to use the gizzard, heart and liver. The gizzard requires thorough cleaning and trimming. Make sure the gall bladder is not broken when removing it from the liver, otherwise it will leave a sharp, bitter taste. Now cut them into thin slices and mix them with a little soy sauce, wine and cornflour. Soak the mushrooms in warm water for about 30 minutes, squeeze them dry and discard the hard stalk. Cut each mushroom into 2–3 pieces if large, leave whole if small. Cut the bamboo shoots, greens and spring onions all into roughly the same shape and size. Mix in a bowl about 2 fl oz (50 ml) of the water in which the mushrooms were soaked with the remaining soy sauce and cornflour.

To cook, first heat about 2 tablespoons oil in a hot wok or large frying pan, swirl it about and wait for it to smoke before stir-frying the vegetables with salt for about 1 minute. Remove and keep them on a warm plate while you heat the remaining oil and stir-fry the giblets with spring onions for about 1½ minutes. Now return the cooked vegetables to the pan, continue stirring, and add the water, soy sauce and cornflour mixture. Stir for a few seconds until all the ingredients are coated with a light, clear glaze. Add the sesame seed oil and serve immediately.

As well as combining all the different flavours and textures, this is a very colourful dish combining green, white, black, brown and purple.

o Stir-fried ten varieties (ii) with meats

This is an ideal way of using up leftovers from roast chicken and meat joints.

— ¼ lb (100 g) cooked chicken meat
¼ lb (100 g) cooked meat or ham
¼ lb (100 g) prawns (peeled and cooked)
3–4 Chinese dried mushrooms

2 oz (50 g) bamboo shoots
¼ lb (100 g) green peas
3 eggs
3–4 tablespoons oil
1 teaspoon salt
1 tablespoon light soy sauce
2 tablespoons rice wine or sherry

Dice the cooked chicken and meat (or ham) into small cubes. Do the same with the mushrooms and bamboo shoots. Stir-fry all these together with the prawns and peas for about 1 minute, add salt and wine, then put aside while you heat some more oil, beat up the eggs and make an omelette, breaking it into small pieces before it is set hard. Now return all the other ingredients to the pan and cook them all together for a few more seconds. Add soy sauce and blend everything well. Serve hot.

This dish is even more colourful than the previous one, with the addition of yellow from the egg and pink from the prawns.

This is a very good starter or an excellent accompaniment to wine (both red and white). But if you happen to have some ready-cooked rice handy, then you can turn it into a meal on its own or serve it as a part of a buffet-type meal. For this, proceed as before, but when you have cooked the beaten eggs keep them aside with the rest of the ingredients. Now heat up some oil and reduce the heat when it starts to smoke, stir-fry the cooked rice until all the grains are separate, add a little soy sauce, stir, then return all other ingredients and cook together until they are well mixed. If you like, garnish with a little finely chopped spring onions when serving.

This is a superior variation of the fried rice you can get from most Chinese restaurants known as Yangchow or Special fried rice, and it is very popular, particularly among young people. Of course you can omit the mushrooms or bamboo shoots, or indeed substitute for them any leftovers you happen to have in your kitchen. Just use your ingenuity and make your own blend of ten varieties.

Those who have been to a 'chop suey' type of Chinese restaurant will have found that almost every single dish served there contains the ubiquitous bean sprouts. It is true that bean sprouts are one of the most common ingredients in China since they are not seasonal, but they are regarded there as an everyday, homely type of food which one would not expect to find on the menu of a restaurant, however humble, except as an ingredient in a few particular dishes. The only explanation I can offer for their popularity abroad is that perhaps in earlier days, when authentic Chinese food was rather hard to come by, bean sprouts were so easy to grow that the restaurant cooks, who were not skilled professional chefs in the strict sense, had to rely heavily on bean sprouts to give their dishes the exotic touch that most customers expected. Thus perhaps developed a kind of vicious circle which continues to this day.

What amazes me is that even though fresh bean sprouts are readily available almost everywhere nowadays, thanks to the flourishing of 'chop suey' Chinese restaurants and take-aways, some cookery writers still advise their readers to use canned bean sprouts in their recipes. This is unforgivable, as it is easy to grow your own if you cannot get them fresh from your local supermarket.

Although I must confess that I have never attempted growing them myself (the need never arose), I have often sampled excellent bean sprouts grown by my mother and her friends. You can obtain packets of mung beans from many shops and health food stores, with detailed growing instructions.

o Shredded pork with bean sprouts

I must emphasize again that on no account should you use canned sprouts. They do not have the crispness of texture which, apart from their high content of vitamin C, is the main characteristic of fresh sprouts.

— ½ lb (225 g) fresh bean sprouts
¼ lb (100 g) lean pork

3–4 tablespoons oil
1 tablespoon light soy sauce
1 tablespoon rice wine or sherry
1 teaspoon sugar
1 teaspoon salt

Wash and rinse the bean sprouts in cold water and discard any husks that float to the surface. Shred the pork into thin strips and stir-fry it in a little warm oil. When the colour of the meat changes, add soy sauce, wine and sugar, blend well, and when the juice starts to bubble, dish it out and put it aside.

Next, wash the wok or pan and heat up some more oil. This time wait for it to smoke, then add the salt, followed by the bean sprouts. Stir vigorously so that every bit of sprout is coated with oil. Now return the pork to the pan and cook all together for about 1 minute, stirring constantly. When the bean sprouts start to become transparent and the juice starts to bubble, the dish is done; even slight overcooking will make the sprouts lose their crispness.

o Pork and french beans

French beans (*haricots verts*), also known as string beans, were introduced into China many centuries ago. They have a most delicate flavour. Get them as fresh as you possibly can – if you grow you own, then pick them at the last moment. Of course, runner beans can be substituted.

½ lb (225 g) lean pork
1 tablespoon light soy sauce
1 tablespoon rice wine or sherry
1 teaspoon cornflour
½ lb french beans (or runner beans)
4 tablespoons oil
1 teaspoon salt

Cut the pork into small, thin slices and marinate with soy sauce, wine, sugar and cornflour. Wash the beans; provided they are fresh and young they will not be stringy and will need only topping and tailing. If you are using dwarf beans, leave them whole; snap large ones in half; runner beans should be sliced.

Heat up about 2 tablespoons oil in a hot wok or frying pan, stir-fry the pork for about 1 minute or until the colour of the meat changes, then dish it out and keep it aside.

Now wash and dry the wok or pan, heat up more oil, but this time wait until it smokes before frying the beans with salt, stirring constantly for about ½ minute. Then return the pork to the pan and blend it well with the beans. Add a little stock or water if necessary, but do not overcook or the beans will lose their crispness and the pork its tenderness.

o Pork and cauliflower

According to *Larousse Gastronomique*, the cauliflower is oriental in origin and has been known in Italy since the sixteenth century. But the interesting thing about this is that I was positively told in China that cauliflower was European in origin and was only introduced into China in the seventeenth century. So who is right? Maybe Marco Polo had something to do with this confusion. Anyway, cauliflower as a vegetable is highly regarded in China and is widely cultivated. Oddly enough, the purple variety, broccoli, which I much prefer, is less popular in China.

1 medium-sized cauliflower
¼ lb (100 g) lean pork
1 tablespoon soy sauce
1 teaspoon sugar
1 teaspoon cornflour
4 tablespoons oil
1 teaspoon salt

When choosing cauliflower, make sure it is fresh, with the leaves that curl round the flower bright green and not withered. Keep a few leaves on when cooking, as they add colour and flavour.

First wash the cauliflower under cold water, and cut the flower into sprigs with part of the stalk still attached. Slice the pork and marinate with soy sauce, sugar and cornflour mixed with a little cold water.

Heat about 3 tablespoons oil in a hot wok or frying pan and stir-fry the cauliflower sprigs with salt for about 1½–2 minutes. Add a little stock or water, let it bubble for a while, then dish the cauliflower out.

Now wash and dry the wok or pan, heat up more oil, and stir-fry the pork for about 2 minutes or until done. Then pour it over the top of the cauliflower and serve.

o Shredded pork with Sichuan preserved vegetable

Sichuan (Szechuan) preserved vegetable is made of the root of a vegetable whose texture resembles a radish, pickled with chilli and salt. It is very hot and salty.

¾ lb (400 g) pork
2 teaspoons cornflour
¼ lb (100 g) Sichuan preserved vegetable
3–4 spring onion stalks
3 tablespoons oil
1 tablespoon soy sauce

Choose a cut of pork that is not too lean, and shred it into strips the size of matchsticks, then marinate with the cornflour mixed with about 1 tablespoon cold water. Shred the preserved vegetable into the same-size strips as the pork. Cut the spring onion stalks into short pieces.

Heat the oil in a hot wok or frying pan, stir-fry the pork by separating the strips with a stirrer or chopsticks. When the colour of the meat starts to change, add the spring onions and soy sauce, continue stirring for a few times more, then add the preserved vegetable and cook all together for about 1 minute or until the pork and vegetable are well blended with each other.

If you find this dish too hot or too salty, you can wash the excess chilli from the vegetable in water before shredding.

o Meat slices with spring onions

This recipe originated in Shandong, a province in the north with which Peking cuisine is closely associated, and which is famous for its leek- and onion-flavoured dishes. You can substitute either onions or leeks for spring onions, and use beef or lamb instead of pork; the method is the same.

— ½ lb ((225 g) pork (or beef or lamb)
1 tablespoon soy sauce
1 tablespoon rice wine or sherry
1 teaspoon sugar
1 teaspoon cornflour
½ lb (225 g) spring onions (or onions or leeks)
½ oz (15 g) Wooden Ears
4 tablespoons oil
— 1 teaspoon salt

Cut the meat into thin slices and marinate with soy sauce, wine, sugar and cornflour. Cut the spring onions or leeks into 1 in (25 mm) lengths or, if using onions, slice them into small pieces. Soak the Wooden Ears in water for 20 minutes, discarding the hard stalks if any, and slice them too.

Heat up the oil in a hot wok or pan until smoking and quickly stir-fry the spring onions for a few seconds only (about 1 minute with onions and leeks). Now add the meat and Wooden Ears with salt and, keeping the heat high, continue stirring for about 1½–2 minutes. Serve hot.

o Shredded pork with green peppers

The green pepper or pimento, a native of America, is now cultivated in all parts of the world. Its crunchy texture makes it very popular in China.

½ lb (225 g) pork
1 tablespoon soy sauce
1 tablespoon rice wine or sherry
1 teaspoon sugar
1 teaspoon cornflour
½ lb (225 g) green peppers
4 tablespoons oil
1 teaspoon salt

Shred the pork into thin strips and marinate with soy sauce, wine, sugar and cornflour. Wash the green peppers in cold water, slit them open and discard the seeds and stalks. Shred them into thin strips.

Heat about 2 tablespoons oil in a hot wok or pan, stir-fry the pork for about 1 minute or until the colour of the meat starts to change, remove and keep aside.

Heat the remaining oil until smoking, add the green peppers, stir for about ½ minute, add salt, continue stirring, then add the meat and cook together for another minute at most. Serve hot.

It goes without saying that you can replace the pork with beef or chicken; indeed, instead of green peppers you can use almost any other kind of vegetable. Equally, you need not shred all the ingredients into thin strips – they could be slices of any shape or size you wish, but bear in mind that both the meat and the vegetable should *match* in shape and size.

o Stuffed green peppers

For this recipe, use small, thin-skinned green peppers if possible.

½ lb (225 g) minced pork
2 spring onions, finely chopped
1 slice peeled ginger root, finely chopped
½ teaspoon salt
1 tablespoon soy sauce
1 tablespoon rice wine or sherry

½ lb (225 g) green peppers
1 tablespoon cornflour
3 tablespoons oil

For the sauce:
2 teaspoons soy sauce
1 teaspoon sugar
3 fl oz (75 ml) stock or water

Mix the minced pork with finely chopped spring onions and ginger root, together with salt, soy sauce and wine.

Wash the peppers, cut them in half and remove the seeds. Stuff them with the pork mixture and sprinkle with a little cornflour.

Heat the oil in a pre-heated flat frying pan, put in the stuffed peppers, meat side down, and fry for 2 minutes, gently shaking the pan now and then to make sure the meat is not stuck to the bottom of the pan. Now mix the sauce and add to the pan, bring to the boil, then reduce the heat and simmer for 5 to 6 minutes. Carefully lift the peppers on to a serving dish, meat side up, and pour any remaining sauce over them. Serve hot.

o Pork laurel (mu-shu pork)

Some explanation is needed for the name of this dish. In China we have a tree called *gui*. According to my dictionary, *gui* is called 'laurel' in English, and it is a shrub rather than a tree; but the laurels we have in the garden of our London home never flower at all, while the Chinese laurel is a large tree which produces bright yellow, fragrant flowers in the autumn. The pork in this recipe is cooked with eggs, which give a yellow colour to the dish – hence the name. But to add to the confusion, the Chinese name of this dish is 'mu-shu pork', *mu-shu* being the classical name for laurel (are you still with me?). So you might say that calling it pork laurel is taking poetic licence!

¼ lb (100 g) pork
2 spring onions

3 tablespoons oil
3–4 eggs
1 tablespoon light soy sauce
1 tablespoon rice wine or sherry
¼ teaspoon salt

Choose a piece of pork that is not too lean (spare rib chops would be ideal) and cut it into shreds the size of matchsticks. Cut up the spring onions into shreds the same size.

Heat up about 2 tablespoons of oil in a hot wok or pan, and while waiting for it to smoke, beat up the eggs. Now reduce the heat and lightly scramble the eggs; dish them out before they set too hard.

Now increase the heat to high again, add more oil, and stir-fry the spring onion and pork shreds together for about 1 minute or until the colour of the pork changes. Add the soy sauce and wine, stir for a few more times, then add the scrambled eggs and salt. Continue stirring and add a little stock or water if necessary. Let all the ingredients blend well and serve hot.

Traditionally this dish is used as a filling for thin pancakes (see p.112) or as a topping on a bed of plain rice. Try using a crisp Webb's lettuce leaf instead of pancake as a wrapper – the contrast in textures is quite sensational!

o Pork laurel Shandong-style

This is a superior version of the earlier recipe, with crunchiness of bamboo shoots and Wooden Ears giving it an added texture.

¼ lb (100 g) pork
2 spring onions
¼ lb (100 g) bamboo shoots
½ oz (15 g) Wooden Ears
3 eggs
4 tablespoons oil
½ teaspoon salt
1 tablespoon light soy sauce

1 tablespoon rice wine or sherry
a few drops sesame seed oil

Soak the Wooden Ears in warm water for about 20 minutes. Shred the pork in matchstick-sized segments; do the same with the spring onions, bamboo shoots and Wooden Ears.

Lightly beat the eggs and scramble them in hot oil as described on page 99, dishing them out before they set too hard. Heat up some more oil, stir-fry the spring onions and pork together for a short while, then add bamboo shoots and Wooden Ears with salt, soy sauce and wine. Stir for about 1 minute, adding a little stock or water if necessary. Finally, add the scrambled eggs and sesame seed oil and blend all the ingredients well before serving.

A variation of this recipe is to use dried Tiger Lily (also called 'yellow flower' in Chinese) instead of bamboo shoots. The method of cooking is exactly the same, but of course the flavour and texture will be slightly different.

o Thin pancakes

1 lb (450 g) plain flour
9 fl oz (250 ml) boiling water
about 1 tablespoon vegetable oil

Sift the flour into a mixing bowl and slowly pour in the boiling water mixed with 1 teaspoon of oil, at the same time stirring with a pair of chopsticks or a wooden spoon. Do not be tempted to add any more water than the amount given otherwise the mixture will get too wet and become messy. Knead into a firm dough, then divide the dough into 3 equal portions. Now roll out each portion into a long 'sausage', and cut each sausage into 8 square pieces. Then, using the palm of your hand, press each piece into a flat pancake. Brush one of the pancakes with a little oil, and place another one on top to form a 'sandwich', so that you end up with 12 sandwiches. Now use a rolling pin to flatten each sandwich into a 6 in (150 mm) circle, rolling gently on each side on a lightly floured surface.

To cook, place a frying pan over a high heat and, when it is hot, reduce the heat to moderate. Put one pancake sandwich at a time into the ungreased pan and turn it over when it starts to puff up with bubbles. It is done when little brown spots appear on the underside. Remove the pancake from the pan and very gently peel apart the two layers and fold them.

If the pancakes are not to be served as soon as they are cooked, they can be warmed up, either in a steamer or in the oven, for 5–10 minutes.

The next four dishes are not intended to be served with others as part of a main meal, but are eaten alone as light snacks. Unlike main meal dishes, they are served in individual bowls or plates.

o Yangchow fried rice

Yangchow, or Yangzhou, cuisine of the Yangtze River delta occupies a particularly important position in the development of Chinese cookery. Apart from the well known Lions' heads (p.37) and many noodle dishes, several of the Cantonese *dim sums*, such as 'Shaomai' and steamed dumplings, are all of Yangzhou origin.

As you can well imagine, there are several variations of this recipe. The one given below is only a basic one from which you should be able to substitute or vary the ingredients as you wish.

4 cups cooked rice
¼ lb (100 g) peeled prawns
¼ lb (100 g) cooked pork or ham
¼ lb (100 g) green peas
3 eggs, lightly beaten
2 spring onions
4 tablespoons oil
2 teaspoons salt
1 tablespoon rice wine or sherry

The rice to be used for this recipe should be neither too hard nor too soft: each grain should be separate. Use peeled and cooked prawns, and make sure they are thoroughly defrosted and dry. Dice the meat into small cubes the size of peas and finely chop the spring onions.

Heat a wok over high heat until hot, add about 2 tablespoons oil, and stir-fry the prawns, meat and peas. Add a pinch of salt and the wine, cook for about 1 minute, then set aside in a bowl.

Heat the remaining oil and lightly scramble the eggs. Add the cooked rice, spring onions and salt, stir to make sure that each grain of rice is separated, then add the prawns, meat and peas. Continue stirring for about 1 more minute or until everything is well blended together. Serve hot.

o Fried noodles or chow mein

After chop suey, chow mein (which means 'fried noodles') must be the next most popular Chinese dish among Westerners – apart, perhaps, from sweet and sour pork. Curiously enough, although noodle dishes are widely eaten in China, the famous 'crispy noodles' served in some Chinese restaurants abroad are just as alien to the Chinese as chop suey. How this came about is a complete mystery to me.

However, fried noodles can be very good when properly cooked. They are very quick and simple, and call for no special ingredients once you have got the basics. As with the 'ten varieties' dishes, you could use almost any leftovers to improve the flavour and texture.

— ½ lb (225 g) egg noodles or spaghetti
½ lb (225 g) meat (pork, beef or chicken)
1 teaspoon salt
½ teaspoon sugar
1 teaspoon cornflour
¼ lb (100 g) bamboo shoots
¼ lb (100 g) leaf spinach (or young greens)

4 tablespoons oil
1 tablespoon light soy sauce
1 tablespoon rice wine or sherry
1–2 spring onions, thinly shredded
a few drops sesame seed oil

If you cannot get Chinese noodles, then use spaghetti (or the finer spaghettini) or noodles, tagliatelle or vermicelli. Allow at least 2 oz (50 g) per person. If you are lucky enough to live near an Oriental foodstore or Italian delicatessen, you may be able to get freshly made noodles which taste far better, cooked, than the dried variety.

First, shred the meat into small, thin strips and mix in a pinch each of salt, sugar and cornflour. Then shred the bamboo shoots into thin strips. Wash the spinach leaves or greens and cut them into shreds too. Now cook the noodles in boiling water according to the instructions on the packet. (Normally this would take about 5 minutes, but freshly made noodles will take only 2 minutes or less). Be careful not to overcook them, or they will become soggy. Drain the noodles and rinse in cold water, then drain again.

Heat about 2 tablespoons oil in a hot wok, stir-fry the meat and vegetable together with salt for about 1½ minutes, add the wine and a little cornflour mixed with cold water to thicken the sauce. Remove and set aside to be used as 'dressing'.

Heat the remaining oil until smoking, add the noodles and spring onions, stir like mad to separate them, then add soy sauce and about half of the 'dressing'. Continue stirring for another ½ minute or so, then serve with the remaining 'dressing' on top and garnished with sesame seed oil.

This is a basic recipe for chow mein, and it never fails to please eager eaters, big and small – it is a firm favourite with both my daughters and their friends. Of course you can substitute any of the ingredients as you like: for instance, the meat could be beef, ham, chicken or prawns; the vegetables could be cabbage, lettuce, cucumber, green beans, mange-touts peas, broccoli or asparagus. The thing to remember here is the contrast of texture and colour.

o Noodles in soup

In China, noodles are served in soup (the name for it is *tang mein*) far more commonly than fried. Why this should be so is hard to explain. On the surface, there is little difference in ingredients used in both dishes, and the methods of preparation are practically the same. The recipe given below is again a basic one which you can alter to suit your preference or according to what is available.

½ lb (225 g) meat (pork, chicken or prawns)
1 teaspoon salt
1 teaspoon cornflour
¼ lb (100 g) bamboo shoots
3–4 dried mushrooms, soaked
¼ lb (100 g) leaf spinach (or lettuce etc)
1 spring onion, thinly shredded
½ lb (225 g) egg noodles or spaghettini
1 pt (600 ml) chicken broth or stock
3 tablespoons oil
2 tablespoons light soy sauce
1 tablespoon rice wine or sherry
1 teaspoon sugar
a few drops sesame seed oil
1 spring onion, finely chopped, to garnish

Cut the meat into thin shreds and marinate in a little salt and cornflour. Thinly shred the bamboo shoots, mushrooms, spinach and the spring onion.

Cook the noodles or spaghettini as for the previous recipe. Drain well and place in a large serving bowl; bring the chicken broth or stock to a boil and pour it over the noodles.

Stir-fry the meat and vegetables as for chow mein, only this time pour all the 'dressing' on top of the noodles and garnish with finely chopped spring onions. Serve hot.

Strictly speaking, you are not supposed to serve either of the noodle dishes at a main meal, and definitely not at the same time as rice – just as you would not serve potatoes and spaghetti together. Noodle dishes in China are normally served in between meals as a snack. Traditionally, though, they are always served at birthday celebrations, partly because the length of noodles represents long life to a Chinese mind.

Noodles in soup are sometimes used for medicinal purposes. I remember on many an occasion when I had a cold as a child in China, my nanny would cook me a large bowl of vermicelli – fine noodles – in steaming hot vegetable soup with masses of ground pepper. It had a sharp taste and my eyes would be streaming with tears. But I would always feel much better afterwards. I suppose it had the same effect as an old-fashioned mustard bath!

o Vegetarian noodles in soup

My earliest recollection of the Chinese countryside is of a trip to a Buddhist temple high up in the wooded hills a few miles from Nanchang, my grandparents' home town, south of the Yangtze River. I was about four or five at the time, and my parents had just returned from Europe after an absence of two years or more. There was an atmosphere of joyousness and festivity – it might well have been at the time of Chinese New Year. It was customary to pay a visit to a temple both before and after a long journey, as well as during the New Year celebrations, not so much for religious worship but rather out of a sense of duty, and to carry on the tradition.

What I remember most vividly to this day is not so much the beautiful scenery which was to become very familiar later on in my life, but the delicious vegetarian noodles in soup the monks offered to their guests on that occasion. The taste was quite unlike anything I ever had before, and totally different from what my nanny used to give me for my colds. Imagine my amusement when, thirty years later and more than ten thousand miles away in London, looking through an old manuscript in the British Museum Library I came across this recipe. Again I have left out a few unusual items included in the original.

1 oz (25 g) dried bean curd skin
3–4 dried mushrooms
1 oz (25 g) dried Tiger Lily
½ lb (225 g) fine noodles or vermicelli
3 tablespoons oil
½ teaspoon salt
1 teaspoon sugar
2 tablespoons soy sauce
1 teaspoon cornflour
a few drops sesame seed oil

Soak the dried bean curd skin in cold water overnight or in warm water for about 1 hour, then slice into thin strips. Thinly slice the dried mushrooms, too. (Tiger Lily needs no slicing as it is in thin strips already.) Keep the water in which all these have been soaked to use as stock for the soup.

Boil the noodles as for the previous recipe. Drain well and place them in a large serving bowl. Keep them warm while you quickly stir-fry the vegetables in hot oil for a few seconds. Add salt, sugar and soy sauce. Continue stirring for a few more seconds, then add about 16 fl oz (450 ml) stock and bring to the boil. Finally, mix the cornflour with a little cold water to make into a smooth paste and add to the pan to thicken the soup before pouring it over the noodles. There should not be too much liquid – only just enough to half cover the noodles. Garnish with sesame seed oil before serving.

According to my source, this dish was offered to the Emperor of China on each New Year's Day – traditionally a fast day. I daresay after the rich feasts he had had all the year round this simple dish was a welcome change for his digestive system!

VI

More Meat than Vegetables

Spare ribs in sweet and sour sauce
Fricassée spare ribs
Bean curd *à la maison* (Bean curd for family meals)
Twice-cooked pork
Braised five flowers pork
Braised brisket of beef
Braised beef with tomatoes
Beef in oyster sauce
Red-cooked pork shoulder
Red-cooked mutton
Stir-fried kidney flowers
Kidney flowers with celery
Kidney flowers Sichuan-style
Stir-fried prawns and kidneys
Stir-fried liver with Wooden Ears
Fried liver Sichuan-style
Cantonese braised calf's liver
Chinese hot-pot

See also:
Red-cooked beef (p.27)
Lions' heads (pork meat balls) (p.37)
Fragrant pork (p.57)
Crystal-boiled pork (p.58)
'Agitated' kidney flowers (p.59)
Braised tripe (p.60)

During the four thousand years or so of known Chinese history, the Imperial capital has always been in the northern parts of the country – with the exception of a few brief periods, notably during the Song dynasty when it was at Hangzhou (1127–1279), and the Ming dynasty when it was at Nanjin (Nanking) (1368–1402). The Chinese Emperor was supposed to be the Son of Heaven, and he lived a very enclosed life inside the Imperial Court, which was known as the 'Great Within'; he was entirely isolated from the people of the nation. He seldom ventured out of the Forbidden City at all, and never visited the other parts of his vast empire – except when he was driven out by foreign invasion or rebellion, which happened now again during the course of history.

It was Emperor Ch'ien Lung (1735–95), one of the most distinguished 'cultured' Emperors of the Qing (Manchu) dynasty, who, while making an extensive tour of southern China, broke the ancient tradition by disguising himself as an ordinary citizen and going out without his entourage to mingle with the people in the streets. This was quite unprecedented and soon became a legend. One of the most popular stories told at the time was that Ch'ien Lung was most amazed by the discovery of the simple but delicious food eaten by his subjects, as opposed to the rich and elaborately prepared feasts he was served all the year round at the court. When he returned to Peking he ordered the

Imperial cooks to prepare for him the simple dishes he had enjoyed at the food stores by the roadside; but alas, the 'simple' dishes prepared in the Imperial kitchens no longer had that magical taste he had first experienced.

In a way we have all had similar surprises and disappointments in our own lives. How many times have we heard people complain that a certain wonderful wine they have discovered in the hot sun of the Mediterranean countries never tastes the same back home, and very often people remember certain foods they had in their childhood but somehow can never recapture the flavour in different surroundings. I mentioned in the Introduction to this book the thrill and excitement of my first encounter with sweet and sour spare ribs in a Cantonese restaurant, but I have never tasted anything like them since. No matter how hard I have tried, using a number of different recipes, the results have been always the same – good enough for most people, but never with that original *je ne sais quoi*.

o Spare ribs in sweet and sour sauce

It is pork spare ribs that you use for this recipe; the cut is sometimes known as Chinese or American spare ribs in Britain, since the English spare rib is a quite different cut.

— 1 lb (450 g) pork spare ribs
½ teaspoon salt
½ teaspoon crushed Sichuan pepper (optional)
1 teaspoon sugar
1 tablespoon brandy or rum
1 egg yolk
1 tablespoon cornflour
1 small green pepper, thinly shredded
about 1 pt (600 ml) oil for deep-frying

For the sauce:
2 tablespoons wine vinegar
2 tablespoons sugar

1 tablespoon soy sauce
1 teaspoon cornflour
2 fl oz (50 ml) stock or water

Ideally, each individual rib should be chopped into 2 or 3 small bite-size pieces. If you do not possess a cleaver, ask your butcher to chop the ribs up for you.

Marinate the spare ribs in salt, pepper, sugar and brandy for at least 15–20 minutes. Meanwhile, make a thin batter by blending the egg yolk and cornflour with a little water. Coat each rib with the batter and deep-fry in hottish oil until crisp and golden. Scoop them out with a perforated spoon or strainer, and heat up the oil to boiling, then fry the spare ribs once more – this time not too long, just enough to darken the colour a little.

Pour off the excess oil, leaving about 2 teaspoons. Stir-fry the thinly shredded green pepper for a few seconds, then add the vinegar, sugar, soy sauce and stock or water together with the cornflour for thickening. When this starts bubbling, blend in the spare ribs, mixing and tossing to make sure that each piece of the spare ribs is coated with the sauce. Serve immediately.

You will find this dish quite different from what you are normally served in a run-of-the-mill Chinese restaurant. When cooked properly, the sauce should be bright and translucent, not too sweet and not too sharp. To add a little more contrast to the colour scheme you can use half a green and half a red pepper.

Fricassée spare ribs

Strictly speaking, a fricassée is a French method of preparing chicken in a white sauce. But in English cooking, the term is applied to various kinds of stewing or braising. In this Cantonese method, called *ju* or *chu*, traditionally an earthenware pot is used; but I have found that a cast-iron casserole is equally good, since this dish is cooked on top of the oven. You can use an ordinary saucepan if you like, but it must have a tightly fitting lid. I have often used an electric wok to cook this dish, and the result has always been satisfactory.

1½ lb (680 g) pork spare ribs
1 tablespoon sugar
1 tablespoon soy sauce
2 tablespoons rice wine or sherry
2 teaspoons cornflour
2 cloves garlic
2–3 spring onions
3 tablespoons oil
2 tablespoons crushed black or yellow bean paste
¼ pt (140 ml) stock or water
1–2 green or red chillis (optional)

Chop each individual rib into 2–3 bite-size pieces, or ask your butcher to do this for you. (With this recipe you *can* cook the ribs whole, but they will take longer and also look rather clumsy when serving.) Marinate the pieces with sugar, wine, soy sauce and cornflour.

Crush the garlic and cut the spring onions into 1in (25mm) lengths. Lightly brown the spare ribs in hot oil for about ½ minute, then remove with a perforated spoon or strainer. Next fry the crushed garlic and the white parts of the spring onions in the same oil with crushed bean paste, and at the same time blend in the spare ribs, stirring constantly to make sure all the pieces are well covered with the sauce. Now add a little stock or water and put the lid on tightly. What you have to do here is to listen carefully for the sizzling noise: does it sound too rapid, so that the heat has to be reduced? Or does it sound too weak, perhaps because you have put too much water in or more heat is needed? All this is very important if you want to make this dish perfectly. Anyway, you have to open the lid now and again (not too often, say every 4–5 minutes) and add more of the water or stock until all the liquid is almost completely absorbed. This should take about 15–20 minutes. Add the green parts of spring onions and green peppers just before serving.

This dish should have a wonderful aroma. The meat should not come off the bone too easily, but it should be very succulent.

One of the simple dishes Emperor Ch'ien Lung discovered among the common people was bean curd (tofu). Made from puréed and pressed soya beans, it is exceptionally high in protein and is known in China as 'poor man's meat'. It is widely used in everyday home cooking and is most useful in absorbing and harmonizing the flavour of other ingredients. It has a rather unusual texture, and is an acquired taste which may not appeal to everybody immediately.

There is an almost endless variety of dishes in which bean curd can be used. The dish that Emperor Ch'ien Lung supposedly liked best is known as 'bean curd for family meals'. You could say it is a sort of chop suey, for it is a bean curd based dish with bits of meat and fish or any leftovers thrown in. My personal favourite is this simple recipe from Sichuan:

o Bean curd *à la maison* (Bean curd for family meals)

4 cakes bean curd
¼ lb (100 g) pork
¼ lb (100 g) young leeks or spring onions
about 1 pt (600 ml) oil for deep-frying
3–4 dried red chillis
1 tablespoon rice wine or sherry
1 tablespoon soy sauce
2 tablespoons crushed yellow bean paste
½ teaspoon cornflour
a few drops sesame seed oil

Split each cake of bean curd into three thin slices crossways, then cut each slice diagonally into two triangles. Cut the pork into thin slices and the leeks or spring onions into ½in (12mm) lengths, also diagonally. Cut the red chillis into small pieces.

Heat up the oil and deep-fry the bean curd pieces for about 2 minutes or until light gold; remove and drain. Pour off excess oil, leaving about 1 tablespoon in the wok. Stir-fry the pork and chillis, add the wine and soy sauce, stir for a few seconds, then add leeks or spring onions, crushed bean paste and bean curd. Stir gently to blend everything together and add a little stock or water if necessary. Finally add the cornflour mixed with a little water to thicken the sauce. Serve garnished with sesame seed oil.

Of course, you can replace the pork with almost any meat you like, or indeed, you can use more than one variety at the same time – it all depends on what you have readily available: prawns, cooked ham, small bits of leftovers from your Sunday joint, etc. To make the dish more colourful, a little green vegetable will be an excellent addition. Just use your initiative and be experimental.

o Twice-cooked pork

Like hot and sour cabbage, this is another Sichuan dish that has become popular throughout China. Any leftovers from crystal-boiled pork (p.58) can be used instead of fresh meat.

1 lb (450 g) belly pork, or any other cut of pork
¼ lb (100 g) bamboo shoots
2–3 spring onions
2–3 tablespoons oil
1 tablespoon crushed yellow bean paste
1 tablespoon chilli bean paste
1 tablespoon rice wine or sherry
1 tablespoon soy sauce
1 teaspoon sugar

Place the piece of pork whole in a saucepan and cover it with water. Bring it to the boil and let it simmer for about 40 minutes, then turn off the heat and leave the meat in the liquid for at least 2–3 hours under cover before removing it to cool with the skin side up.

Meanwhile, cut the bamboo shoots into small slices and spring onions into ½in (12mm) lengths. Skin the pork, and if you are calorie conscious, cut off some of the excess fat. Slice the meat into thin pieces about the size of large postage stamps.

Heat the oil in a hot wok or frying-pan, throw in the spring onions followed by the bean paste, stir for a couple of seconds, then add the pork and bamboo shoots together with wine, soy sauce and sugar. Stir for about 1½ minutes, adding a little water or stock if necessary.

You can substitute the bamboo shoots with any other seasonal vegetable, in which case stir-fry the fresh vegetable first for a few seconds before adding the pork to the pan.

o Braised five flowers pork

In China this is the most popular way of cooking pork. If you cook more than you need for one meal, the rest can be warmed up and served again or used as an ingredient for a number of recipes.

1½ lb (680 g) belly pork
2 spring onions
2 slices peeled ginger root
1 teaspoon oil
4 tablespoons rice wine or sherry
4 tablespoons soy sauce (1 of light and 3 of dark)
1 tablespoon sugar
1 teaspoon Five Spice powder
some vegetables (optional)

Cut the pork into 1in (25mm) cubes, the spring onions into ½in (12mm) lengths, and the ginger root into 2 or 3 small pieces.

In a warm greased pan, brown the pork lightly, then add the spring onions, ginger root, wine, soy sauce, sugar and Five Spice powder with enough water to cover the meat. Bring it to the boil and skim the surface. Now place a tightly fitting lid on the pan, reduce the heat, and let it simmer gently for 1½ hours.

You can serve the dish on its own or add, in the last 30 minutes of cooking, some vegetables such as cabbage, carrots, turnips, bamboo shoots or bean curd, mushrooms (fresh or dried), all of which will help to absorb the fat from the meat as well as improve the flavour.

o Braised brisket of beef

As I mentioned earlier, beef is regarded as inferior to pork in China, so brisket of beef is about the lowest of the low! However, if you follow this recipe you will end up with a nourishing, delicious and economical dish.

1½ lb (680 g) brisket of beef (or shin shank)
1 tablespoon sugar
2 tablespoons oil
3 spring onions, finely chopped
4 slices peeled ginger root, finely chopped
4 tablespoons soy sauce (1 of light and 3 of dark)
3 tablespoons rice wine or sherry
1 teaspoon Five Spice powder

Trim the beef of excess fat, but do not overdo this as the fat helps to enrich the juice and keep the meat tender. Cut the beef into 1in (25mm) squares, or longer chunks of the same width.

Bring to the boil 1½ pt (850 ml) of water and parboil the beef chunks rapidly for 3 minutes. Now turn off the heat (if you cook by electricity then remove the saucepan from the cooker), and scoop out the beef with a perforated spoon.

Put 1 tablespoon of sugar in the water: after about 10 minutes, all the impurities will sink to the bottom of the pan leaving the stock clear. Drain it through a fine sieve and keep it aside.

Heat the oil in a hot wok or large frying pan, and stir-fry the finely chopped spring onions and ginger root, followed by the parboiled beef with the soy sauce, wine and Five Spice powder. Stir for a few minutes, then transfer back to the saucepan and add the stock. Bring to the boil, put on the lid, turn down the heat, and let it simmer gently for 1½–2 hours; by then the juice should be reduced to less than ½ pt (280 ml) and have become a rich, brown sauce with a wonderful aroma.

You can either serve it immediately, in which case skim off the excess fat, or let it cool and then de-fat and reheat it the next day.

Any cheap cuts of mutton (such as breast or stewing mutton) can be cooked in the same way, but perhaps increasing the amount of spring onions and ginger root.

o Braised beef with tomatoes

Another way of cooking the cheaper cuts of beef is this recipe from Tianjin (Tientsin) in northern China. You will find this dish a pleasant change from plain stewed beef, and well worth the extra effort.

1½ lb (680 g) stewing or braising beef
1 lb (450 g) tomatoes
3 oz (75 g) sugar
2 spring onions
2 cloves garlic
2 slices peeled ginger root
2 tablespoons oil
2 tablespoons soy sauce
2 tablespoons rice wine or sherry
1 teaspoon cornflour
salt and pepper to taste

Place the beef, cut into large pieces, in a saucepan and cover it with cold water. Add a spring onion, a clove of garlic and a slice of ginger root. Bring to the boil and simmer gently with a tightly fitting lid for about 1½ hours. Add more water freely during the course of cooking.

Skin the tomatoes by plunging them in boiling water for a short while, then cut them into small pieces and stew them with about 2 oz (50 g) of sugar in another saucepan until they become almost a purée-like liquid.

Scoop out the beef when it is done, let it cool a little. Then cut it into small squares. Fry the beef in hot oil for a few seconds, then remove it, leaving a little oil in the pan. Throw in 1 crushed clove of garlic, let it turn golden, then add 1 finely chopped spring onion, 1 slice of ginger root, the wine and soy sauce, 1 oz (25 g) sugar and about ½ pt (280 ml) stock from the meat. Blend well, add the beef and bring it to the boil; then reduce the heat and cook gently for 5 minutes. Drain off any excess juice, add the tomatoes, and cook a further 2–3 minutes. Just before serving, thicken the sauce by mixing in a little cornflour and adjust seasonings.

Needless to say, any leftovers can be reheated and will taste just as good the next day.

o Beef in oyster sauce

The Chinese are fond of combining sharply contrasted flavours in a way that would seem highly unusual to a Westerner – as in the dish of kidneys and prawns cooked together (p.138). One of the most successful of these combinations is this famous Cantonese dish of beef cooked in oyster sauce.

Oyster sauce is by no means a luxury in China, since it is only soy sauce with oyster flavouring. It should cost not much more than the best soy sauce, and a small bottle will go a long way as you need only a little at a time.

½ lb (225 g) frying steak
2 tablespoons oyster sauce
1 teaspoon sugar
1 tablespoon rice wine or sherry
1 teaspoon cornflour
1–2 spring onions
2 slices peeled ginger root
1 small Chinese cabbage or cos lettuce
4 tablespoons oil
1 teaspoon salt

Cut the beef into thin slices across the grain, mix with the oyster sauce, sugar, wine and cornflour and marinate for about 1 hour.

Cut the spring onions into 1in (25mm) lengths and cut the ginger root into small bits. Wash the cabbage and cut each leaf into 2 or 3 pieces. If you are using a cos lettuce, discard the tough outer leaves and tear (do not cut) the larger leaves into 2 or 3 pieces, leaving the small inner leaves whole.

Heat about 2 tablespoons oil in a hot wok or large frying pan, wait for it to smoke, then stir-fry the cabbage or lettuce with salt. Stir constantly until the leaves become limp – this will take 1½–2 minutes for the cabbage, but less than 1 minute for lettuce. Remove quickly and place on a serving dish.

Wipe the wok or pan clean with a damp cloth and heat the remaining oil until very hot. Add the spring onions and ginger root followed by the beef, stirring vigorously for about 30 seconds at most, then dish it out quickly as soon as the colour of the beef changes. Serve hot on the bed of cabbage or lettuce.

Do not overcook the beef unless you like your steak to be tough; and watch the heat, keeping it as high as you can manage all the time.

o Red-cooked pork shoulder

This is a famous dish from southern China, a must for any festivity, big or small; I suppose it is the nearest equivalent to a traditional Sunday joint in Britain.

1 pork shoulder (3½–4 lb/1.6–1.8 kg)
4–6 spring onions
6 tablespoons soy sauce (2 of light and 4 of dark)
3–4 tablespoons rice wine or sherry
3 tablespoons crystallized (or brown) sugar
1 teaspoon Five Spice powder
some vegetables (optional)

Pork shoulder sometimes is known as hand of pork in England and as picnic shoulder in the USA (a more expensive cut is the leg part known as knuckle in England or ham in the USA). It is usually sold with the bone in and the rind on.

Before cooking, blanch it by placing the whole piece of pork in cold water and bringing it to the boil for a few minutes, then discard the water and rinse the pork under the cold tap.

Now place the meat in a large pot, add the spring onions, soy sauce, wine, sugar, Five Spice powder and about 1 pt (600 ml) cold water. Cover it with a tightly fitting lid and bring it to the boil over high heat, then reduce the heat and let it simmer gently for 2½ hours, turning it over carefully several times during cooking. There should be very little liquid left at the end; if necessary, turn up the heat and cook uncovered until the liquid is reduced and has become rather thick.

Traditionally, the pork is served whole in a large bowl with the juice poured over it. Sometimes root vegetables such as carrots or bamboo shoots are added during the last 30 minutes of cooking to absorb some of the fat. When it is done perfectly, the rind and meat should be soft enough to be pulled off the bone with a pair of chopsticks or a fork. Any leftovers can be cut into slices and served cold.

o Red-cooked mutton

This is a very simple way of cooking the cheaper cuts of mutton or lamb – or indeed any type of meat. It can be cooked the day before, then warmed up and served whenever you require.

1½ lb (680 g) mutton or stewing lamb
3 tablespoons rice wine or sherry
2 slices ginger root
1 teaspoon Sichuan peppercorns
3–4 tablespoons soy sauce
1 tablespoon sugar
1 clove garlic, crushed
1 teaspoon sesame seed oil (optional)

First wash the meat thoroughly in cold water, then dip it in boiling water for a short while before cutting it into small squares. Now place the meat pieces in a saucepan and add wine, ginger root and peppercorns together with enough stock or water to cover. Bring to the boil, then reduce the heat and simmer for 1 hour under a tightly fitting lid. Add the soy sauce, sugar and crushed garlic. Cook for a further 30 minutes or until almost no juice is left, and then it is ready.

A Chinese housewife who set out to do her daily shopping each morning seldom has a preconceived idea as to what sort of food she will be buying, for much depends on what she will find when she gets to the market. Her prime consideration will be the quality and freshness of the food – and also the value for money. As a small child, I used to accompany my nanny to the market every morning on my way to kindergarten. To get the best and freshest meat and vegetables, you had to be really early, for by mid-morning there would be hardly anything to choose from except a few pathetic-looking remnants.

I used to enjoy these shopping expeditions enormously. I would help my nanny to pick and choose, and sometimes even bargained for her, to the great amusement of the vendors and storekeepers. My wife thinks that is probably why I have such an eye for bargains when we go out shopping together now.

A market-place in China was a bustling and noisy place. Besides the permanent stores, there were dozens of makeshift stands where the peasants from the outskirts of the town would bring in their farm produce to sell – the chickens and ducks were always alive and kicking, and the fish always swimming in water. All the vegetables were so fresh that you could still see morning dew on them, since they were truly dawn-picked only a few hours earlier. I learned from my nanny how to distinguish the freshly picked vegetables from ones that had been picked the day before and had been artificially kept 'fresh' by soaking in water all night.

Years later, when my parents lived in Oxford, there was the covered market in the centre of the city, not unlike the one I knew in China, but there was no early morning rush, no live poultry or fish, and no vegetables that one would really call fresh.

Later still, on the Continent, I came across several markets which recaptured a little of the Chinese atmosphere, but alas, one's childhood memories linger on!

For the rest of this chapter, I shall offer a selection of slightly unusual dishes using ingredients which, though easily obtainable, may have been ignored by cooks who are not sure how best to deal with them. Do not, however, be disappointed when you discover that there are no recipes for such exotic items as bird's nest soup or shark's fins: their ingredients are very expensive to buy and tedious to prepare, and besides, they are definitely not everyday, homely food so there is no place for them in this book.

I have already mentioned the use of giblets (p.101), but not the wide use of offal or the variety of meats used in Chinese cooking. Nothing edible is thrown away in China. In the case of pork, not only the kidneys, liver, brains, trotters and head are considered delicacies, but also all the entrails and the blood are very much used. Because of their reputedly extra nutritive value, some butchers in certain parts of China would charge for items such as kidneys and liver *more* than for the best 'ordinary' cuts of meats. On the other hand, in the part of the country we lived in during the war with Japan, the butchers had to force the customers to take some offal as a makeweight with their purchases of meat.

o Stir-fried kidney flowers

If ever I were a castaway on a desert island, the one non-fish dish I should miss most would undoubtedly be this. Kidney dishes have always been among my favourites, and this one is my favourite of all. The recipe comes from Shandong. For years it was on the menu in a Chinese restaurant in Paris, but the last time I went there, with my family, to our great disappointment the restaurant had changed hands and our favourite dish was no longer served there.

— 1 pair pork kidneys (about ½ lb/225 g)
2 oz (50 g) water chestnuts

2 oz (50 g) bamboo shoots
½ oz (15 g) Wooden Ears
¼ lb (100 g) seasonal green vegetable (lettuce, cabbage or spinach)
1 spring onion, finely chopped
1 clove garlic, finely chopped
1 slice peeled ginger root, finely chopped
about 1 pt (600 ml) oil for deep-frying
1 teaspoon salt
1 tablespoon cornflour
1 tablespoon wine vinegar
1 tablespoon soy sauce
1 tablespoon rice wine or sherry

Pork kidneys should be bright reddish-brown in colour; do not buy any that have turned dark purple, or that do not smell fresh. First peel off the thin white skin covering the kidneys (if the butcher has not already done so), then split them in half lengthways and discard the fat and white, tough parts in the middle. Score the surface of the kidneys diagonally in a criss-cross pattern and then cut them into medium-sized pieces so that when cooked they will open up and resemble ears of corn – hence the name of this dish. Marinate with a pinch of salt and about ½ tablespoon cornflour mixed with a little water.

Slice the water chestnuts and bamboo shoots. Soak the Wooden Ears in warm water for about 20 minutes and discard the hard parts. Blanch the green vegetables and finely chop the spring onion, garlic and ginger root.

Heat the oil in a wok or deep saucepan until very hot, deep-fry the kidney pieces for a few seconds only, stir with a wooden-handled carving fork to separate the pieces, then quickly scoop them out with a perforated spoon.

Pour off the excess oil, leaving about 2 tablespoons in the pan. Now fry the finely chopped spring onion, garlic and ginger root. Add the vinegar, followed by water chestnuts, bamboo shoots, green vegetable, Wooden Ears and kidneys, then add soy sauce and wine. Stir a few times, and, finally, add the cornflour mixed with a little stock or water. Blend everything well and serve hot.

This dish should have a harmonious balance of aroma, texture and colour, and is ideal for acccompanying wine even though it has a touch of vinegar in it.

o Kidney flowers with celery

This is a Cantonese recipe and needs slightly less preparation than the previous one.

1 pair pork kidneys (about ½ lb/225 g)
1 tablespoon soy sauce
1 tablespoon rice wine or sherry
1 medium-sized head celery
3–4 spring onions
1 clove garlic
2 slices peeled ginger root
1 teaspoon sugar
1 teaspoon cornflour
4 tablespoons oil
1 teaspoon salt
a few drops sesame seed oil (optional)

Prepare the kidneys as described in the previous recipe. Marinate them in the soy sauce and wine. Wash the celery and cut it diagonally, giving it half a turn between each cut so that the pieces are diamond-shaped. Cut the spring onions into 1in (25mm) lengths and finely chop the garlic. Make a thin paste by mixing the sugar and cornflour with a little stock or water.

First stir-fry the celery with the salt in about 2 tablespoons hot oil, then put it aside. Now heat up the remaining oil and throw in the garlic, ginger root slices and spring onions, followed by the kidneys. Stir for a short while, then add the celery. Blend everything well before adding the paste mixture, then bring to the boil, stirring all the time. If desired, a few drops of sesame seed oil may be added just before serving.

o Kidney flowers Sichuan-style

This is a hot and sour version of kidney flowers, as its origin suggests. Both the bamboo shoots and dried mushrooms called for in this recipe can be substituted, as the main character of the recipe comes from the piquant sauce rather than the supplementary ingredients used.

1 pair pork kidneys (about ½ lb/225 g)
¼ lb (100 g) bamboo shoots (or carrots, courgettes, asparagus, etc)
5–6 dried mushrooms (or ¼ lb/100 g fresh mushrooms)
3–4 dried red chillis
2 spring onions
2 slices peeled ginger root
1 clove garlic
1 teaspoon salt
1 tablespoon rice wine or sherry
1 teaspoon cornflour
¼ teaspoon ground Sichuan pepper
about 1 pt (600 ml) oil for deep-frying

For the sauce:
1 tablespoon soy sauce
1 tablespoon wine vinegar
1 tablespoon sugar
2 teaspoons cornflour mixed with a little water

Prepare the kidneys as for previous recipes and marinate the pieces with a pinch of salt, pepper, wine and cornflour. Cut the bamboo shoots and mushrooms (or their substitutes) into slices. Cut the chillis into small bits, discarding the seeds unless you like your food really hot. Finely chop the spring onions, ginger root and garlic. Mix the sauce.

First deep-fry the kidneys for about 30 seconds in hot oil, then quickly scoop them out with a perforated spoon and drain. Pour off the excess oil, leaving about 2 tablespoons in the wok or pan. Put in the red chillis to flavour the oil, then add garlic, ginger root and spring onions followed by the vegetables and kidneys. Stir for a few times, then add the sauce. Blend everything well, and serve as soon as the sauce starts to bubble.

This is the most piquant and delicious dish, typical of Sichuan cuisine in that you are served several flavours (sweet, salt, sour and hot) all at once.

o Stir-fried prawns and kidneys

Having given you recipes for kidneys from the north (Shandong), south (Canton), and west (Sichuan), now it is the turn of eastern China, and in this case Shanghai. You may think the idea of combining prawns and kidneys is rather strange, but the Chinese believe this technique of mixing two entirely different ingredients helps to promote an exchange of flavours, each ingredient acquiring a new flavour and at the same time acting as a seasoning agent on the other. It is a matter of 'give and take', rather as in a well-matched marriage – though one must not get too philosophical about it – all part of the *yin-yang* principle (see p.183).

¼ lb (100 g) peeled prawns or shrimps
½ lb (225 g) pork kidneys
½ egg white
1 tablespoon cornflour
1 teaspoon salt
2 oz (50 g) bamboo shoots (or carrots, celery, etc)
3–4 dried mushrooms (or ¼ lb/100 g fresh mushrooms)
about ¼ lb (100 g) seasonal green vegetable (lettuce, cabbage, spinach, etc)
1–2 spring onions
4 tablespoons oil
1 tablespoon soy sauce
1 tablespoon rice wine or sherry
1 teaspoon sugar
a few drops of sesame seed oil

Clean and dry the prawns, marinate with egg white and about 1 teaspoon cornflour mixed with a little water. Prepare the kidneys as for previous recipes, and marinate with a pinch of salt and a little cornflour and water mixture. Cut the vegetables into small slices, and the spring onions into short lengths.

Heat up about 2 tablespoons oil in a hot wok or large frying pan, and quickly stir-fry the prawns and kidneys for a very short while – about 1 minute at very most – stir to separate the pieces, then scoop them all out with a perforated spoon.

Heat up the remaining oil and stir-fry the spring onions first, then the rest of the vegetables with a little salt; stir for about another minute then add the prawns and kidneys together with soy sauce, wine and sugar. Now add the remaining cornflour and water mixture, stir a few more times, and add a dash of sesame seed oil just before serving.

Stir-fried liver with Wooden Ears

Pig's liver is held in high regard in China for its nutritive value. Because of its delicate texture, it should never be overcooked; when it is done in this quick stir-fried way, even young children who normally dislike 'liver and bacon' relish it.

This dish is the most popular way of serving pig's liver in China. The contrast between the crunchiness of the fungus and the tender smoothness of the liver makes it extremely palatable.

1 oz (25 g) Wooden Ears
½ lb (225 g) pig's liver
2 spring onions
3–4 tablespoons oil
1 tablespoon soy sauce
1 teaspoon cornflour
½ teaspoon salt

Soak the Wooden Ears in warm water for about 20 minutes, then rinse in cold water. Tear the large ones into smaller pieces and discard any hard stalks. Wash the liver, discard the white membranes and cut it into medium slices about ⅛ in (3 mm) thick. Place the slices in a large bowl. Cut the spring onions into ½in (12mm) lengths.

Heat up the oil in a hot wok or pan. While waiting for it to smoke, quickly pour some boiling water over the liver, stir to separate each piece, then drain away the water and mix the liver with soy sauce and cornflour. Now add the liver to the hot oil and stir 4–5 times before adding the spring onions and Wooden Ears together with the salt; stir-fry for about 30 seconds, then it is ready. The crucial point here is timing and heat; provided you keep cool during the whole operation it is comparatively simple: just remember not to overcook but keep the heat as high as you possibly can.

o Fried liver Sichuan-style

This is a slightly simpler way of cooking liver. As with most Sichuan dishes, the emphasis is on the piquant sauce, and you can substitute the vegetable quite freely, replacing bamboo shoots with any other that has a crunchy texture: Wooden Ears, celery, green peppers, etc.

— 1 lb (450 g) pig's liver
¼ lb (100 g) bamboo shoots (or celery, courgettes, etc)
2 spring onions
2–3 slices peeled ginger root
about 5 tablespoons oil
1 teaspoon salt
½ teaspoon ground Sichuan pepper
1 tablespoon rice wine or sherry
2 teaspoons cornflour
a few drops sesame seed oil

For the sauce:
1 clove garlic, crushed and finely chopped
1 tablespoon soy sauce
1 tablespoon rice wine or sherry

1 tablespoon sugar
1 teaspoon cornflour mixed with a little water

Clean and cut the liver into small, thin slices and marinate with salt, pepper, wine and cornflour.

Slice the bamboo shoots or other vegetables and finely chop the spring onions and ginger root. Prepare the sauce by mixing all the ingredients together in a jug or bowl.

Heat the oil in a hot wok or pan until smoking, stir-fry the liver for a few seconds, then quickly scoop it out with a perforated spoon. Now fry the spring onions and ginger root with the bamboo shoots or other vegetables; stir for about 30 seconds then add the partly cooked liver, stir a few times, then add the ready-mixed sauce and continue stirring. When all the ingredients are well blended it is done. Just before serving, add a few drops of sesame seed oil and more pepper. The dish should have a lovely fragrance and texture.

○ Cantonese braised calf's liver

This delicious Cantonese dish also has the fuller name of 'braised calf's liver with ginger and onions', and it is quite easy to cook.

¾ lb (340 g) calf's (or ox) liver
½ teaspoon salt
½ teaspoon ground pepper
1 teaspoon sugar
1 tablespoon soy sauce
1 tablespoon rice wine or sherry
1 teaspoon cornflour
1 large onion
4 spring onions
5–6 slices peeled ginger root
1–2 cloves garlic
3 tablespoons oil

For the sauce:
1 tablespoon oyster sauce
1 tablespoon soy sauce
1 tablespoon rice wine or sherry
1 teaspoon cornflour mixed with a little stock or water

Cut the liver into thin slices and marinate with salt, pepper, sugar, soy sauce, wine and cornflour for about 30 minutes.

Thinly slice the onion, cut the spring onions into ½in (12mm) lengths, thinly shred the ginger root and crush the garlic.

Heat the oil in a hot wok or deep pan, and stir-fry the onion, garlic and ginger root followed by the liver for about 30 seconds. Now add the sauce and spring onions, bring to the boil, and braise under cover for about 1–1½ minutes, and it is done.

o Chinese hot-pot

Now for something completely different: here is an unusual way of preparing Chinese food in which the actual cooking is done not in the kitchen but at the dinner table, and is very much a do-it-yourself affair.

You can get a charcoal-burning hot-pot from most Chinese stores. It may seem to be a large outlay, and for years my wife and I had doubts about its usefulness before we eventually bought one; but I can assure you that it is a sound investment, besides looking most attractive and impressive on the table. There is nothing more warming on a cold winter's day than to catch a drift of burning charcoal and see the steaming pot bubbling with its delicious contents. It never fails to delight our guests, and our children claim that it is the most fun way of serving a meal.

Also known as 'Mongolian fire pot', this dish is not unlike a fondue; stock or plain water is brought to the boil over a charcoal burner on the centre of the table and everybody cooks his or her own food in it. Originally, only mutton or lamb was used (as is still the case in the restaurants in Peking), but nowadays there is no strict rule as to what ingredients you must or must not use and they vary enormously from place to place or according to seasonal availability – but it is definitely a winter dish, just as a barbecue is only for the summer.

As for the dip sauce, there could be as many as 15 different ingredients used, although the number is much reduced when the dish is served as an everyday meal at home.

The quantity I have given should be enough for at least six to eight people. This is a complete meal on its own; I do not think you will need anything else to go with it – apart from a bottle, or two, of good wine, of course.

1 lb (450 g) leg of lamb fillet (or pork, beef, or all three)
½ lb (225 g) chicken breast fillet
½ lb (225 g) peeled prawns
½ lb (225 g) fish fillet (or squid, or both)
¼ lb (100 g) pork or chicken liver
¼ lb (100 g) pork or lamb kidneys
2 oz (50 g) dried mushrooms (or ½ lb/225g fresh mushrooms)
1 lb (450 g) Chinese cabbage (or spinach)
2–3 cakes bean curd
1 lb (450 g) fine noodles or vermicelli (optional)
about 3–4 pt (1.7–2.3 litres) stock or water

For the dip:
4–6 tablespoons soy sauce
1 tablespoon sugar
3–4 spring onions, finely chopped
3–4 slices peeled ginger root, finely chopped
2 teaspoons sesame seed oil
chilli sauce (only for those who like it)

Cut the meats and fish into as thin slices as you possibly can and arrange them either on a large plate or put them on small individual dishes. Soak the dried mushrooms in warm water for ½ hour or so, then discard the stalks and cut the mushrooms into thin slices. Wash the cabbage or spinach and cut it into small pieces. Cut the bean curd into small pieces, and arrange all the vegetables neatly, either together or separately, like the meats.

Mix all the ingredients for the dip sauce, pour it into 4–6 little dishes and place them on the table within easy reach of everyone.

All these preparations should be done beforehand. Now first bring the stock or water to a fast boil. Each person then picks up a piece of meat of his or her choice with chopsticks (or a fork) and dips it in the boiling liquid for a very short time – usually as soon as the colour of the meat changes it is done – then quickly retrieves it, dips it in sauce and eats it while still piping hot.

When all the meats have been eaten, add the remaining vegetables to the pot, let boil vigorously for a minute or two, then ladle out the contents into individual bowls. Add the remains of the dip sauce and serve as a most delicious soup to finish off the meal.

VII

Fish without Chips

Braised fish steak
Fried fish fingers
Fried fish slices
Red-cooked carp
Steamed whole fish
Crab with spring onions and ginger
Fu-yung crab meat
Fried prawns with mange-touts peas
Prawns in shells
Sesame seed prawn toast
Scallops with mixed vegetables
Fish slices and mushrooms assembly
Sweet and sour fish
Fish-head soup

See also:
Stir-fried prawns and peas (p. 40)
Fish-slices soup (p.52)
'Smoked' fish (p.61)
Phoenix tail prawns (p.62)
'Agitated' prawns (p.63)
Stir-fried prawns and kidneys (p.138)

In China, fish is far more widely eaten than meat, partly because of its abundance which makes it comparatively less expensive. This tendency is not confined only to the regions along the coastline, but in all other parts inland where there are plenty of freshwater fish from rivers, lakes and ponds. In the countryside, ponds are not just used as reservoirs for agriculture, but for extensive fish farming as well.

I was rather puzzled when I first came to England and observed that although surrounded by sea, the British treated fish with distrust. It took me a little while to discover the explanation – to start with, I think most people have childhood memories of poorly prepared fish dishes that have left (literally) a bad taste. And in the days before ready prepared and attractively packaged frozen fish was widely available on the market, an average housewife who was confronted with a vast variety of species, some glowering at her with strangely shaped heads, would naturally feel alarmed and confused.

Nowadays, the old fashioned type of fishmonger's is disappearing fast to make way for the streamlined supermarket where one can usually find a fresh fish counter alongside the frozen packets, so the choice is wide. The fishmonger – old or new style – is generally very accommodating; he will clean and scale the fish and leave it whole, or skin and fillet it for you, as you wish; so all you have to do is find a good recipe and do the cooking without being bothered by the more tedious task of preliminary preparation.

The most important thing to look for when choosing fish is its freshness. I think it is not generally appreciated that fish is more perishable than meat or poultry and, ideally, fish and shellfish should be kept alive until just before cooking, as we do in China. Efficient refrigeration on board modern fishing vessels may keep the fish reasonably fresh for a few days after its capture, but once it has been landed it is kept chilled by being packed in ice during its journey to market and while it is on the fishmonger's slab. By the time you have brought the fish home from the fishmonger do not expect it to keep fresh more than a few hours even if it is stored in your refrigerator. Deep-freezing is no solution, as it significantly affects the flavour and texture of the fish – the flesh loses its springiness, and cooking only makes it dry, tough and tasteless. It is only natural that the greater the time that elapses between the fish being taken from the water and its appearance at the table, the less fresh it will be.

A few years ago, when I returned home from Ireland after conducting a short course on Chinese cookery as a guest tutor at the Ballymaloe Cookery School, Co. Cork, my very first words to my family who greeted me was that I wanted to go and live in Ireland. 'For two reasons,' I declared to a puzzled but attentive audience. 'The first reason: the grey mullet!' The whole assembly – there were friends there as well as the family – just collapsed with laughter: they couldn't believe that I was serious, and in the ensuing hilarity no one asked me for the second reason, which was because of the live shrimps and prawns!

It is a sad reflection on the 'progress' of modern society that those of us who live in it rarely get food as fresh as that eaten by those in less industrialized societies. All this was brought home to me during my trip to southern Ireland. Situated in the middle of a 400-acre farm, Ballymaloe House is owned and run by the Allen family. The Cookery School, which is located two miles away in a beautiful Regency house one mile from the sea, is run by Darina Allen, a daughter-in-law of Myrtle Allen, who developed the Ballymaloe style of cooking using the natural produce of the surrounding area. The orchards and extensive vegetable and herb gardens of the school, and the abundance of seafood from the nearby fishing village of Ballycotton, supply much of the fresh ingredients used both at the school and in the restaurant at Ballymaloe.

The evening of my arrival at Ballymaloe, Darina told me that she had just got some fresh shrimps for my demonstration the next morning, and asked should she cook them straight away for me as she was worried that they would not be still alive the next day? Now since I have not been able to obtain live shrimps for more than thirty years, I urged her to keep them alive for me until the next day, which she duly did by going all the way back to Ballycotton Bay to fetch a bucket of seawater in order to keep the shrimps fresh for me. On another occasion, when I expressed my doubt about using plaice for one of my recipes, remembering the rather poor quality species one was accustomed to in Britain, Darina reassured me that the flavour of the fish would be delicious, as it would be freshly caught from a small boat with a small trawl (much of the delicate flavour is lost when the fish is taken from a big trawler as it gets bruised in the big catch during its long journey at high sea). Of course she proved to be right. The biggest surprise for me was the grey mullet which was good enough reason for my wanting to go and live in Ireland.

Recently I went back to Ballymaloe. This time I took my wife with me, and she agreed wholeheartedly with my reasons for wanting to live in Ireland. What accounts for the excellent food is, of course, the freshness of the ingredients used. Both Myrtle and Darina believe, essentially, that good food must be treated with respect and prepared to enrich and enhance, but never mask, its true natural flavours. I quote Myrtle Allen from her delightful *The Ballymaloe Cookbook* (Gill and Macmillan): 'The thing that matters most about fish is its freshness. The extreme urgency of getting fish from the sea to table is not properly appreciated. I can't see why anybody living within 200 miles of the coast should have to eat fish that is more than 36 hours out of the sea, since we no longer depend on horse transport. Refrigeration is no help, if only used for holding fish in storage longer.'

o Braised fish steak

This is an excellent way of cooking cod or haddock cutlets, or halibut (very expensive), or monkfish tails (usually good value). The most important thing to remember apart from freshness is that the flesh of most fish is very delicate, and if cooked too long over too high a heat it will lose its flavour and texture. Treat fish like the tenderest cuts of beef or veal.

1 lb (450 g) fish steak
1 tablespoon cornflour
1–2 spring onions
1 slice peeled ginger root
about 1 pt (600 ml) oil for deep-frying
2 tablespoons rice wine or sherry
2 tablespoons light soy sauce
1 tablespoon sugar

Do not remove the skin from the fish, and do not cut it into too small pieces or they will break easily during cooking. Dry the fish thoroughly with a cloth or kitchen paper and coat each piece with cornflour blended with a little water. Finely chop the spring onions and ginger root.

Heat the oil in a hot wok or pan until moderately hot, then reduce the heat and fry the fish pieces until light golden. Remove and drain. Pour off excess oil, leaving about ½ tablespoon in the pan. Now increase the heat to high again and throw in the ginger and onions, followed almost immediately by the fish pieces. Shake the pan, turning the fish pieces over very gently to make sure they are cooked evenly. Now add wine, soy sauce, sugar and a little stock or water. Bring to the boil, then reduce the heat and simmer for 5–6 minutes depending on the type of fish you use, or until the juice is almost entirely evaporated. Just before serving, mix about 1 teaspoon cornflour with a little water and pour it over the fish as you bring up the heat again to thicken the sauce.

o Fried fish fingers

Are you surprised by the name of this dish? Strictly speaking, it is called 'fish stripes' in Chinese, but I thought 'fish fingers' sounded more homely. In fact, you could use a packet of frozen fish fingers for this recipe; it will save you a lot of preparation and the result will be almost as good for it is the sauce that makes the dish.

¾ lb (340 g) fish fillets (or 14–16 fish fingers)
1–2 spring onions
1 slice peeled ginger root
1 clove garlic
plain flour or breadcrumbs for coating
about 1 pt (600 ml) oil for deep-frying

For the sauce:
1 tablespoon soy sauce
1 tablespoon rice wine or sherry
1 tablespoon vinegar
1 tablespoon sugar
1 teaspoon cornflour mixed with a little stock or water

Use cod or haddock or any other white, firm fish that you can cut into long, thin strips like fingers. Cut the spring onions into short pieces about 1 in (25 mm) long, and finely chop the ginger root and garlic.

While you wait for the oil to heat up, coat the fish 'stripes' with flour or breadcrumbs. Reduce the heat before you put the fish in the hot oil, otherwise they will burn before they are cooked. Deep-fry them until they are golden, then remove and drain.

Now pour off excess oil, leaving about ½ tablespoon in the pan, and first fry the garlic, ginger root and spring onions for a few seconds. Then add the fish fingers, followed by the sauce mixture. Stir gently until everything is well blended. The fish should be crispy outside and tender inside, and I promise you ordinary fish fingers taste like something exceptional from an expensive restaurant!

o Fried fish slices

After fish steaks and fish fingers, perhaps you would like to try fish slices for a change. To save you the bother of cutting fish into thin slices, you could use fillets of flat fish such as plaice or sole.

¾ lb (340 g) fish fillets
1 egg white, lightly beaten
1 tablespoon cornflour
1 clove garlic, crushed and finely chopped
1 spring onion, finely chopped
about 1 pt (600 ml) oil for deep-frying
1 teaspoon salt
1 teaspoon sugar
3–4 tablespoons rice wine or sherry
4 fl oz (125 ml) stock or water
a few drops sesame seed oil (optional)

Cut the fish into large slices, leaving the skin on. Mix them first with the egg white and then the cornflour blended with a little water into a smooth paste.

Heat up the oil in a very hot wok or pan, but before it becomes too hot, reduce the heat, add the fish slices one by one, reserving the leftover cornflour paste, and fry gently for about 1 minute using a pair of chopsticks or a wooden-handled carving fork to separate each slice. Scoop them out with a perforated spoon and drain.

Pour off the excess oil, leaving about 2 teaspoons in the pan.

Add the garlic and spring onion to flavour the oil, followed by the fish slices. Add salt, sugar, wine and the stock or water. Turn the heat up high and bring the sauce to boil. Tilt the wok or pan and turn round slowly at an angle so that the sauce covers the fish evenly. Finally, add the remaining cornflour and water mixture very slowly to thicken the sauce, then garnish with sesame seed oil. Serve hot. (Try not to break up the slices when sliding them out on to a serving dish.)

Smaller fish under 2 lb (900 g) in weight are best cooked whole. If you can get freshwater fish such as carp, perch, bream or trout, so much the better; if not, sea bass, sea bream, grey mullet or grouper will do just as well, only their meat is not quite so delicate as that of freshwater fish.

I must again emphasize the importance of freshness when choosing fish. The usual rules are that its eyes should be clear and full, not sunken; that its gills should be bright red; that the body should be firm, not flabby; and that it should smell pleasantly fresh and not have a disagreeable odour.

In China, apart from the vegetarians, everyone eats meat, but there are quite a number of people who dislike fish as food. My father is one of them, while my mother positively preferred fish to meat, and the rest of the family seems to be divided half and half – with myself strongly on my mother's side. I was told that when my mother was expecting me she had a craving for freshwater fish, which happened to be rather short in the market in Peking that winter, and I have always believed that was why I like fish so much. One day, when I was about six or seven years old and was travelling with my nanny on one of the small inland rivers in China, the boatman caught a beautiful carp (or was it a perch? I cannot be sure). He cooked it for our lunch, and it was the tastiest fish I have ever eaten. To this day I can still recall vividly the simply cooked fish with its delicious sauce, but everything else about the journey I have completely forgotten, except that I remember my nanny remarked afterwards that nothing could excel river fish cooked with river water. How right she was!

o Red-cooked carp

The commonest freshwater fish in China must be the carp, and red-cooking must be about the most usual method of cooking any fish. Carp is a beautiful silver-grey fish. It has become the symbol of good fortune, so it is a must for the traditional New Year celebrations, wedding feasts or any other festivity.

The carp was first imported into Britain in the early seventeenth century and was not introduced into the USA until 1876, but it has since become very abundant there. It is also a favourite fish with Jewish and Central European cooks, and is now widely bred in special farms in Israel.

The ideal weight of the carp for this recipe is about 1½ lb (680 g) or a little more. It is cooked whole with its head and tail on. Ask your fishmonger to clean and scale it for you if you are not sure how to do it yourself, and try to cook it the day you buy it as it does not keep well – this, of course, applies to all freshwater fish.

1 carp (or perch, trout, sea bass, grey mullet etc), 1½–2 lb (680–900 g)
2 spring onions
2 slices peeled ginger root
4–5 tablespoons oil

For the sauce:
3–4 tablespoons soy sauce
3–4 tablespoons rice wine or sherry
1 teaspoon sugar
about 2 fl oz (50 ml) stock or water

Scale and gut the fish (if not already done), wash it under the cold tap and dry it well both inside and out with a cloth or kitchen paper. Trim the fins and tail if not already trimmed, and slash both sides of the fish diagonally as far as the bone at intervals of about ½ in (12 mm) with a sharp knife. In case you wonder why it is necessary to slash both sides of the fish before cooking, the reason is twofold: first, if you cook the fish whole, the skin will burst unless it is scored; and second, it allows the heat to penetrate more quickly and at the same time helps to diffuse the flavours of the seasoning and sauce. Also, as the Chinese never use a knife at the table, it is much easier to serve the fish if you can pick up pieces of flesh with just a pair of chopsticks.

Cut the spring onions into 1 in (25 mm) lengths, and cut the ginger root into thin shreds. Mix the ingredients of the sauce in a bowl.

Heat up a wok or pan until hot, add the oil and wait for it to smoke before frying the fish for about 2 minutes on each side. Now remove some of the oil, leaving about 1 tablespoon, push the fish to one side and throw in the spring onions and ginger root, followed by the sauce mixture. Move the fish back to the centre and bring the sauce to the boil. Cook for about 5–6 minutes, basting the fish constantly and turning it over once or twice.

Serve the fish on an oval-shaped dish – and do be careful not to break the fish for not only will it look bad, it will not taste the same either!

o Steamed whole fish

In China the perch is considered one of the best freshwater fish. Its flesh is more delicate than that of the carp, and in flavour it resembles salmon trout. There is a different species in America, called perch trout, and another relative is the sea bass. (The word 'bass' is derived from 'barse', the old English name for the perch.) In this recipe you can use either sea bass or salmon trout if perch is not available.

1 perch (or sea bass, salmon trout etc) 1½–2 lb (680–900 g)
1 teaspoon salt
1 teaspoon sesame seed oil
4 spring onions
2–3 dried mushrooms, soaked and thinly shredded

2 oz (50 g) pork fillet or cooked ham, thinly shredded
2 tablespoons light soy sauce
1 tablespoon rice wine or sherry
2 slices peeled ginger root, thinly shredded
2 tablespoons oil

Clean, trim and slash the fish as in the previous recipe. Rub about half the salt and all the sesame seed oil inside the fish, and place it on top of 2–3 spring onions on an oval-shaped dish.

Mix the mushrooms and pork with the remaining salt, a little of the soy sauce and wine. Stuff about half of this mixture inside the fish and the rest on top with the ginger root. Place in a hot steamer and steam vigorously for 15 minutes.

Meanwhile, thinly shred the remaining spring onions and heat the oil in a little saucepan until bubbling. Remove the fish dish from the steamer, arrange the spring onion shreds on top, pour the remaining soy sauce over it and then the hot oil from head to tail. Serve hot.

If you don't possess a steamer big enough to hold a whole fish, it can be wrapped in silver foil and baked in the oven at 450°F (230°C), gas mark 8 for 20–25 minutes.

Fresh and seawater shellfish are, as you can well imagine, highly thought of in China. The most common ones are prawns, shrimps and crabs.

The season for crabs is rather short (usually from May to September). Choose a crab which is not too small, otherwise there will be more shell than meat in proportion to its size – but if it is too large, the meat tends to be tough. The female, or 'hen', crabs contain a yellowish roe rather like the yolk of an egg, called the 'berry' in England. This is highly appreciated in China for its characteristic crab flavour. But unfortunately the crab meat you buy in a tin or frozen packet has had this delicious roe removed. When you buy a fresh crab from the fishmonger, and if you are lucky enough to pick out a hen crab, ask him to crack open the body and claws for you and make sure you get the berry.

o Crab with spring onions and ginger

This is an excellent way of cooking crab in its shell. It is best accompanied by a fino or medium-dry sherry, for ordinary table wine has not the strength to sustain this highly flavoured dish.

2 medium-sized crabs (about ¾ lb/680 g each)
4–5 spring onions
4–5 slices peeled ginger root
2 eggs
¼ teaspoon salt
3–4 tablespoons oil
2 tablespoons light soy sauce
2 tablespoons rice wine or sherry
1 teaspoon sugar

Break off the legs and crack the claws of the crabs if the fishmonger has not already done so. Wash off any mud or green matter both outside and inside the shell, and discard the feathery gills.

Cut the spring onions into 1 in (25 mm) lengths, finely chop the ginger root and beat up the eggs with a little salt.

Heat the oil in a hot wok or large pan, wait for it to smoke and then fry the crabs, stirring constantly for about 1 minute or until the colour turns bright red. Add the spring onions, ginger root, soy sauce, wine and sugar, and continue stirring for another minute or so. Then pour the beaten eggs all over the crabs, stir gently and serve just before the eggs become solid.

o Fu-yung crab meat

As explained on p.83, the term 'fu-yung' in Chinese means 'lotus-white', because only the white of eggs is used to make the dish. This famous Peking dish originally called for the white of the eggs with the 'yolk' of the female, or hen, crab. Since it is rather difficult to get hold of crab 'yolk' nowadays, I have taken the liberty of adapting the recipe somewhat by using the white crab meat and keeping in the yolk of the eggs – there is real compromise for you!

½ lb (225 g) crab meat
6 eggs, with the whites and yolks separated
1 teaspoon salt
2 spring onions, finely chopped
1 slice peeled ginger root, finely chopped
3 tablespoons oil
1 teaspoon sugar
1 tablespoon rice wine or sherry

If you are using frozen crab meat, make sure it is defrosted at room temperature for at least 4 hours – never try the short-cut method of soaking it in hot water, which will spoil much of its delicate flavour. For this recipe you can even use canned crab meat; in this case drain it and discard the soft little bones.

Break up the meat into small pieces and mix it with the yolks of the eggs. Finely chop the spring onions and ginger root. Lightly beat up the whites of the eggs.

Heat up the oil in a hot wok or pan, and throw in the spring onions and ginger, followed by the crab meat. Add salt, sugar and wine, stir for about 30 seconds, then pour the egg whites over and blend them well to a creamy consistency. Do not overcook, particularly if you are using canned crab meat.

o Fried prawns with mange-touts peas

Fresh prawns and shrimps are grey and almost translucent until cooked, when they turn bright pink. The larger variety, known as Pacific or king prawns, are usually sold in their shells without the heads; the smaller ones are usually sold peeled and frozen or in brine. You may have difficulty obtaining them, but only *uncooked* prawns are suitable for this recipe.

The mange-tout, also known as snow pea or sugar pea, is at its best from spring to late summer. If you are unable to obtain it, then substitute any other green vegetable such as french beans, broccoli or green peppers.

½ lb (225 g) uncooked prawns
½ egg white, lightly beaten
1 teaspoon cornflour blended with a little cold water
½ lb (225 g) mange-touts peas (or any other seasonal greens)
1 slice peeled ginger root
4 tablespoons oil
1 teaspoon salt
1 teaspoon sugar
1 tablespoon rice wine or sherry
a few drops sesame seed oil (optional)

Wash and shell the prawns. Dry them thoroughly with kitchen paper, then use a sharp knife to make a shallow incision down the back of each prawn and pull out the black intestinal vein. Cut each prawn in half if large, leave them whole if small. Mix the prawns first with the egg white, then the cornflour and water mixture, and blend well with your fingers.

Wash the mange-touts in cold water. If the pods are picked as soon as they are formed, they will not be stringy and will only need to be topped and tailed. Cut the ginger root into small bits.

Put a wok or pan over a high heat, and when it is hot put in the oil and heat it until moderately hot. Now reduce the heat to low and let the oil cool down a little before frying the prawns for about 10–15 seconds only. Stir to separate them, then quickly scoop them out with a perforated spoon. Now increase the heat to high again and wait for the oil to smoke. Add the ginger root followed by the mange-touts, stir for about 1 minute, then add the prawns with salt, sugar and wine. Stir a few more times, add sesame seed oil (if using), then it is done. The vegetable should be bright and crisp, and the prawns so tender as almost to melt in your mouth.

Prawns in shells

A popular dish from Shanghai which can be served cold and is ideal for 'wine-accompanying'. You will find that even a red wine (but not one that is too delicate) can be served with this dish.

½ lb (225 g) uncooked Pacific or king prawns
2 spring onions, finely chopped
2 slices peeled ginger root, finely chopped
about 1 pt (600 ml) oil for deep-frying
2 tablespoons soy sauce
2 tablespoons rice wine or sherry
1 tablespoon sugar
1 lettuce heart
fresh coriander or parsley to garnish

Wash and trim off the legs of the prawns but keep the body shells on. Dry thoroughly. Deep-fry them in hottish oil for a few seconds only, and as soon as they start to turn pink, quickly scoop them out with a perforated spoon.

Pour off the oil, then return the prawns to the pan and add the soy sauce, wine and sugar with the finely chopped spring onions and ginger root. Stir vigorously for a little while until each prawn is coated with the glittering sauce, then it is done.

Arrange the prawns neatly on a bed of lettuce leaves and garnish with fresh coriander or parsley. When eating, you put the whole prawn in your mouth, suck the sauce and at the same time extract the meat from the shell. This is easily done if you use chopsticks rather than a spoon or fork. If your guests are unfamiliar with chopsticks, then urge them to use their fingers instead.

Sesame seed prawn toast

Those of you who have been to a Chinese restaurant serving Peking-style food will probably have been delighted by this delicious dish. It is in fact quite simple and easy to make, and would no doubt equally delight, and impress, your guests.

½ lb (225 g) uncooked prawns
2 oz (50 g) fresh pork fat
1 teaspoon salt
pepper to taste
1 egg white, lightly beaten
1–2 spring onions, finely chopped
1 slice peeled ginger root, finely chopped
1 tablespoon rice wine or sherry
2 teaspoons cornflour
6 large slices white bread, with crusts trimmed
¼ lb (100 g) white sesame seed oil
about 2 pt (1.1 litres) oil for deep-frying

Wash, shell, dry and de-vein the prawns as in the previous recipes. Chop the prawns and pork fat together until they form a smooth paste, then mix with the salt, pepper, egg white, finely chopped spring onion and ginger, wine and cornflour. Blend everything thoroughly.

Spread the sesame seeds evenly on a large plate or a baking tray. Now spread the prawn mixture very thickly on the top of each slice of bread, then place the slices, spread-side down, on the surface of the sesame seeds. Press gently so that each slice has a good coating of seeds.

Heat the oil in a wok or deep-fryer until hot, fry the slices of bread, spread-side down, 2 or 3 slices at a time, for about 2 minutes or until they start to turn golden; then turn them over and fry for a further minute or so. Remove and drain on absorbent kitchen paper.

Cut each slice into 6 fingers or 4 triangles, and serve hot. They should taste wonderful – 'Out of this world', as my young children would say!

A mixture of breadcrumbs and sesame seeds can be used for the coating. It will still taste delicious, though not with quite the same aroma.

○ Scallops with mixed vegetables

This is a very colourful and delicious dish. Try to get the large queen scallops that contain the orange roe. When fresh scallops are out of season, prawns can be cooked in exactly the same way, you can use a mixture of both to enhance the flavour, as is often done in some Cantonese restaurants.

4–6 fresh scallops
½ egg white, lightly beaten
2 teaspoons cornflour mixed with about 1 tablespoon water
2–3 stalks celery
1 red pepper, cored and seeded
1–2 carrots
1 slice peeled ginger root
2–3 spring onions
4 tablespoons oil
1 teaspoon salt
1 teaspoon sugar
1 tablespoon rice wine or sherry
1 tablespoon light soy sauce
1 teaspoon chilli bean paste
a few drops of sesame seed oil

Cut each scallop into 3–4 thin slices, mix with the egg white and about half of the cornflour and water mixture.

Cut the celery, red pepper and carrots into pieces roughly about the size of a postage stamp. Cut the ginger root into small bits and the spring onions into short lengths.

Heat the oil in a very hot wok or pan until fairly hot, then reduce the heat and let the oil cool down a little before stir-frying the scallops for about 30 seconds and scooping them out with a perforated spoon. Now increase the heat to high again. Add the ginger root and spring onions followed by the vegetables. Stir for about 1 minute, then return the scallops to the pan and add salt, sugar, wine, soy sauce and the chilli bean paste. Stir a few more times, then add the remaining cornflour and water mixture.

Blend all the ingredients well, and as soon as the sauce starts to thicken, add the sesame seed oil. Serve hot.

Fish slices and mushrooms assembly

This dish is not unlike the French 'Filets de Sole Bonne Femme' (sole with mushrooms and wine sauce), but I think you will agree that the Chinese method is much simpler.

1 lb (450 g) fillet of sole (or other flat fish such as plaice, flounder, brill etc)
1 egg white, lightly beaten
1 tablespoon cornflour mixed with a little water
½ lb (225 g) fresh white mushrooms
2–3 spring onions
1 slice peeled ginger root
1 pt (600 ml) oil for deep-frying
1 teaspoon salt
1 teaspoon sugar
1 tablespoon light soy sauce
1 tablespoon rice wine or sherry
4 fl oz (125 ml) good stock or water
a few drops sesame seed oil (optional)

Trim off the soft bones along the edges of the fish, but leave the skin on. Cut each fillet into 3–4 pieces if large, 2–3 pieces if small. Mix with the egg white and cornflour.

Thinly slice the mushrooms, and thinly shred the spring onions and ginger root.

Heat the oil until hot, then reduce the heat and let the oil cool down a little before frying the fish slices for about 1 minute at most, using a pair of chopsticks to stir gently to make sure the pieces are not stuck together. Remove and drain.

Pour off the excess oil, leaving about 2 tablespoons in the pan. Now turn up the heat to high again. Add the spring onions, ginger root and mushrooms, stir a few times, then add the salt, sugar, soy sauce, wine and stock or water. Bring to the boil. Now add the fish slices and simmer for about 1–1½ minutes. Finally thicken the sauce with what is left of the cornflour and water mixture, garnish with sesame seed oil and serve hot.

o Sweet and sour fish

Fish cooked whole always looks impressive, and is a must for any feast, big or small. It is usually served in a rich sauce and with dressings of one kind or another – for this is the cook's chance of showing off his or her skill in presentation: it is the *pièce de résistance.*

1 carp (or sea bass or grey mullet) 1½–2 lb (680–900 g)
1 teaspoon salt
about 2 tablespoons plain flour
*1 green pepper, cored and seeded
*1 carrot
*1–2 sticks celery
2–3 spring onions
2 slices peeled ginger root
1 clove garlic, crushed
5–6 tablespoons oil
2–3 tablespoons vinegar

**Or:*
2 oz (50 g) bamboo shoots
3–4 water chestnuts
a few Wooden Ears (soaked)

For the sauce:
3 tablespoons sugar
2 tablespoons soy sauce
2 tablespoons rice wine or sherry
1 teaspoon chilli sauce (optional)
2 teaspoons cornflour
¼ pt (140 ml) stock or water

Clean, scale and score the fish as described in the earlier whole fish recipes (pp. 154, 155). Dry it thoroughly with a cloth or kitchen paper before rubbing it with salt both inside and out, then coat the whole fish from head to tail with flour.

Thinly shred the green pepper, carrot and celery (or bamboo shoots, water chestnuts and Wooden Ears previously soaked in warm water for about 20 minutes). Shred the spring onions and ginger root to the size of matchsticks, and finely chop the garlic. Mix all the ingredients of the sauce.

Heat the oil in a hot wok or large frying pan until smoking, and fry the fish for about 3–4 minutes on both sides, or until golden and crisp. Be very careful when turning the fish over, and use a wide-bladed tool to remove it from the pan so that it is kept in one piece. Drain and place the fish on a heated long dish.

Pour off the excess oil, leaving about 2 tablespoons in the pan. Fry the spring onions, ginger root and garlic, followed almost immediately by the vegetables. Stir and add the vinegar, then add the sauce mixture, stirring constantly until the sauce thickens. Pour the vegetables with the sauce over the fish and serve immediately.

o Fish-head soup

It is fitting and traditional to end a banquet with a dish that is simplicity itself. Nothing is simpler or easier to make than this soup, which is made out of the remains of the main course of the feast.

Head, tail and leftovers from a whole fish
1 pt (600 ml) stock
1 pt (600 ml) water
1 spring onion, finely chopped
1 teaspoon vinegar
salt and pepper to taste
fresh coriander or parsley to garnish

Traditionally, the fish head and tail are used with any other leftovers from sweet and sour fish. First break up the bone and crush the head into smaller pieces, add to the stock and water, bring to the boil and simmer for a few minutes.

To serve, place the finely chopped spring onion in a large bowl, pour the boiling soup over it, adjust seasonings, and garnish with fresh coriander or parsley. Served hot, it is most delicious!

Of course you should have no difficulty in choosing a suitable wine for any of these fish dishes. As everybody knows, white wine goes best with fish, but do not rule out the possibility of red altogether. For instance, a cool, fresh Beaujolais will go very nicely with most of these dishes, and the more strongly flavoured dishes such as the red-cooked carp, crab with spring onion and ginger, and sweet and sour fish all require something a little fuller than ordinary table wine. I suggest that you try a fino or medium-dry sherry. A Manzanilla or Amontillado is very similar both in taste and body to the Chinese 'yellow wine' made of glutinous rice, which is the most popular drink in many parts of China. For further suggestions on wines to drink with Chinese food, see Chapter X.

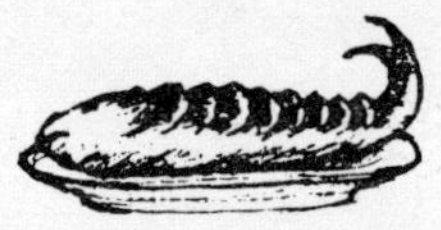

VIII

First Catch Your Duck

Roast duck Peking-style
Gold and silver duck
Duck liver in wine sauce
Duck giblets assembly
Braised duck
Roast duck Canton-style
Aromatic and crispy duck
Duck soup

If I were asked to name one single dish as the best example of *haute cuisine* in China, the choice would be difficult but after a little hesitation I would eventually decide on Peking duck.

This unique dish owes its worldwide reputation not so much to the way it is cooked, which can be very simple, but also to the way it is eaten. Another important factor lies in the specially reared species of duck used. To start with, it has a different appearance from the common duck and is brought by several stages of force-feeding and care to exactly the right degree of plumpness and tenderness before it is prepared for the oven.

As you will realize, Peking duck is, strictly speaking, not a home dish but, since most Western kitchens are equipped with an oven, there is no reason why you should not try to cook it at home. The original Chinese recipe runs on for pages, starting with a detailed description of how to make up the duck feed, and continuing with complicated instructions on how to build and fire the oven. There is also an important aspect of the preparation: the killing of the duck. It starts off, literally, with 'First catch your duck'! Then it goes on to say: 'With your left hand get hold of both wings of the duck, using your little finger to hook up the right foot of the duck, meanwhile using your thumb and index finger to press down on the duck's neck; and with the knife in your right hand . . .' I think I will spare you the rest of the gory details.

Since it is almost impossible to obtain everything you need for genuine Peking duck outside China, I have modified the Chinese recipe somewhat, and I can assure you that the result is entirely satisfactory.

o Roast duck Peking-style

1 duckling, 4½–5 lb (2–2.3 kg)

For cooking (optional):
1 tablespoon sugar
1 teaspoon salt
½ pt (280 ml) water

For the sauce:
3 tablespoons yellow bean paste
2 tablespoons sugar
1 tablespoon sesame seed oil

**or* substitute 6 tablespoons Hoi Sin sauce

For serving:
24 thin pancakes (see p.112)
10 spring onions
½ cucumber

Try to get a fresh (not frozen) oven-ready duckling not less than 4 lb (1.8 kg) in weight: the smaller the duck, the less the meat, but if the duck is over 5 lb (2.3 kg) the meat will be too tough.

In order to make the skin appear golden as well as crispy, it is advisable to coat the duck with a mixture of sugar, salt and water before drying. To do this you mix 1 tablespoon sugar with 1 teaspoon salt in ½ pt (280 ml) water and rub the duck with this mixture.

There is very little else to do except to clean the duck and hang it up to dry thoroughly, preferably overnight in a draught (or use a fan heater or even a hairdryer). It is most important to ensure that the duck is dry, as the drier the skin the crispier the duck when roasted, and crispness is one of the main characteristics of this dish.

When the duck is thoroughly dry, place it on the middle rack of a preheated oven (400°F/200°C, gas mark 6) and roast for just over 1 hour 10 minutes – add an extra 10 minutes for every extra 1 lb (450 g) over 4½ lb (2 kg).

While the duck is being roasted (there is nothing to be done to it, no basting or turning over), you can make the thin pancakes, using the recipe on p.112, and the sauce. The sauce is simply made by mixing the crushed yellow bean sauce, sugar and sesame seed oil over a gentle heat for 2–3 minutes. Next thinly shred the spring onions into 2in (50cm) lengths and slice the cucumber into thin strips of the same length. All these accompaniments are served in separate dishes, and the duck is carved at the table, with the skin and meat in separate dishes.

To eat, you help yourself to a pancake, and on it you spread a teaspoon or so of sauce, then place a few cucumber and spring onion strips in the middle, and on top of these you place a piece or two of the sliced duck meat with a piece or two of the crispy skin. Now roll up the pancake like a sausage roll, turning up the bottom end to prevent anything dropping out.

The combination of the crunchy vegetables, the crispy skin and the tender meat with the sweet sauce is indescribable.

The carcass of the duck is crushed to make a soup with cabbage and is served at the end of the meal (p.177). There is very little waste in cooking a duck: almost everything can be used in a number of delicious dishes. (One of the duck restaurants in Peking offers more than a hundred different dishes on the menu, entirely based on parts of duck. But most of these are far beyond our scope; for instance, one recipe calls for thirty duck tongues!)

o Gold and silver duck

This is an ideal way of using up any leftovers from the roast duck – though you are most unlikely to have any, unless your guests failed to turn up! The main ingredients of this dish are cooked duck meat and ham: the pale colour of the duck offsets the pinkness of the ham, forming a pretty pattern when arranged on a serving plate – hence the name of this dish.

½ lb (225 g) cooked duck meat
½ lb (225 g) cooked ham

2 teaspoons gelatine
2 tablespoons rice wine or sherry
¼ pt (150 ml) stock or water
salt and pepper to taste

Slice both duck and ham into thin pieces of roughly the same size – say not larger than a matchbox – and arrange them alternately in several layers on a deep, long dish. Sprinkle them with a little salt and pepper. Dissolve the gelatine in hot stock or water with the wine. (It is important to make sure the gelatine is completely dissolved as otherwise the jelly will not set; detailed instructions are normally given on each packet of gelatine.) Pour it all over the duck and ham, and refrigerate until set. Turn it out on to another long dish for serving either as an hors d'oeuvre or as a part of a buffet meal.

o Duck liver in wine sauce

This is another cold dish, and therefore ideal for serving as a starter or as what the Chinese call a 'wine-accompanying' dish.

1 lb (450 g) duck liver
2 tablespoons rice wine or sherry
2 tablespoons brandy
1 tablespoon sugar
1 teaspoon salt
1 tablespoon soy sauce
7 fl oz (200 ml) stock or water

Wash and clean the liver well, trimming off any part that has been discoloured by the gall bladder. Place the liver in a pan, cover with cold water and bring to the boil, then drain and discard the water. Next return the liver to the pan, add the wine, brandy, sugar, salt, soy sauce and stock or water, and bring it to the boil. Simmer gently for about 10 minutes, then take the liver out to cool.

To serve, cut the liver into thin slices and arrange them in neat rows on a plate. Pour over the remains of the sauce, which should have been reduced to no more than couple of tablespoons.

o Duck giblets assembly

The ingredients for this recipe are not unlike those of 'Stir-fried ten varieties (i)' (p.101), but the method is somewhat different.

giblets (gizzards and hearts only) from 2–3 ducks (or chickens)
¼ lb (100 g) bamboo shoots
4–6 dried mushrooms, soaked (or ¼ lb/100 g fresh mushrooms)
1 cos lettuce (or ½ lb/225 g green cabbage)
3–4 tablespoons oil
1 teaspoon salt
1 tablespoon soy sauce
1 tablespoon rice wine or sherry
1 teaspoon cornflour mixed with a little water

Slit the gizzards on the curved side, open them and remove the inner bags, taking care not to break them as they are full of grit. Sometimes this has already been done, so all you have to do is clean and wash the gizzards well. Trim off the excess fat from the upper parts of the hearts.

First place the giblets in cold water and bring to the boil, then plunge them in cold water before cutting them into thin slices.

Slice the bamboo shoots, mushrooms, lettuce or cabbage. If using fresh mushrooms, blanch them; also blanch the lettuce or cabbage, drain and put them aside.

Next heat the oil in a hot wok or pan until hot, add the giblets with bamboo shoots, mushrooms and greens, stir for a few times, then add salt, soy sauce and wine. Continue stirring for about 1 minute, adding a little stock or water if necessary. Finally, thicken the gravy with the cornflour and water mixture so that the finished dish has a translucent glaze.

o Braised duck

In China, duck is second only to chicken in popularity as a poultry dish. While chicken is more of an everyday food, duck is something special, a must for festivities and feasts. As I mentioned earlier, not many Chinese homes are equipped with a Western-type oven, and therefore stewing or braising is by far the most widely used cooking method for poultry in China.

1 duckling (4½–5 lb/2–2.3 kg)
2–3 spring onions, finely chopped
2–3 slices ginger root, finely chopped
1 teaspoon Five Spice powder
5 tablespoons soy sauce (2 of light and 3 of dark)
4 tablespoons rice wine or sherry
¼ lb (100 g) rock candy or crystallized sugar

Clean the duck thoroughly and place the finely chopped spring onions and ginger root together with the Five Spice powder inside the cavity of the duck.

Use a large saucepan or a casserole to boil about 2 pt (1.1 litres) of water, put in the duck and boil rapidly for 4–5 minutes, turning it over once or twice. Then discard two-thirds of the water and add the soy sauce, wine and candy or sugar. Bring back to the boil, then put on the lid tightly and simmer gently for 30 minutes, turning the duck over at least once. At this stage you can either continue cooking over a low heat for 1 hour longer or transfer the casserole to a preheated oven (375°F/190°C, gas mark 5) for 1 hour.

Either serve the duck whole in its own juice, or take it out, chop it into bite-size pieces (see p.68), and serve hot or cold.

o Roast duck Canton-style

Those of you who have been to a good Cantonese restaurant must have tasted those delicious roast ducks seen hanging in the windows. They have a shining reddish-brown skin and are often called 'lacquered ducks'. Strictly speaking, they are not really part of home cooking in China; but since almost every kitchen in the West is equipped with an oven, there is no reason why you should not enjoy this luxury by serving it at your banquet.

1 duckling (4½–5 lb/2–2.3 kg)
1 teaspoon salt

For the stuffing:
1 tablespoon oil
2 spring onions, finely chopped
2 slices peeled ginger root, finely chopped
2 tablespoons sugar
2 tablespoons rice wine or sherry
1 tablespoon crushed yellow bean paste
1 tablespoon Hoi Sin sauce
1 teaspoon Five Spice powder

For coating:
4 tablespoons honey
1 tablespoon vinegar
½ pt (280 ml) water
a little 'red powder' (or cochineal)

Wash and clean the duck well, then pat it dry inside and out with a cloth or kitchen paper. Rub it inside and out with salt, then tie the neck tightly with string so that no liquid drips out when the duck is hanging with its head down.

To make the stuffing, heat up the oil in a saucepan, add all the ingredients, bring to the boil and blend the mixture well. Pour it into the cavity of the duck and sew it up securely.

Now make the coating by boiling the water and adding the honey, vinegar and a little colouring. Mix well.

Next plunge the whole duck into a large pot of boiling water for a few seconds only, take it out, and baste it thoroughly with the 'coating' mixture. Hang it up to dry for at least 2–3 hours (use a hairdryer or fan heater to hasten the drying process).

To cook, preheat the oven to 400°F (200°C) gas mark 6.

Hang the duck head down in the oven on a meat hook, and put a tray of hot water at the bottom of the oven to catch the drippings and to create extra steam. After 25 minutes or so, reduce the heat to 350°F (180°C) gas mark 4 and roast for a further 30 minutes, basting with the remains of the mixture once or twice during the cooking. When it is done, let it cool a little, then remove the string and pour out the liquid stuffing (it can be used as gravy).

Traditionally, this duck is chopped into small bite-size pieces (see p.68) and served cold. But there is no reason why you should not serve it whole and carve it at the table, as it looks most impressive with its 'lacquered' skin all glittering.

o Aromatic and crispy duck

Because this dish is on the menu of most Peking-style restaurants, and because it is usually served with pancakes with spring onions and a sweet bean paste, many people mistakenly think this is *the* Peking duck. They can be forgiven for this misconception, since this duck dish originated in Shandong and is believed to be the forerunner of its more illustrious cousin in the restaurants in Peking.

1 duckling (3½–4 lb/1.6–1.8 kg)
2 teaspoons salt
3–4 spring onions
3–4 slices ginger root
*4 star anise
*1 teaspoon cloves
*2 sticks cinnamon
1 tablespoon Sichuan peppercorns
3–4 tablespoons rice wine or sherry
3–4 tablespoons soy sauce
about 2–pt (1.1 litres) oil for deep-frying
1 lettuce heart
**or:* substitute 2–3 teaspoons Five Spice powder

Clean the duck well and trim off the tips of its wings. Split it down the back and rub it with salt on both sides. Marinate in a large bowl with the spring onions cut into short lengths, ginger root, the spices, wine and soy sauce for 4 hours or more, turning it occasionally.

Remove the duck from the marinade and place it in a deep dish inside a large steamer or, if your steamer is not big enough, chop the duck in half lengthwise and steam the two halves on separate layers. Steam the duck vigorously for 3–4 hours, adding more boiling water when necessary. Remove the duck, drain it, and allow to cool for at least 4–6 hours.

Heat the oil in a wok or deep-fryer until smoking. Deep-fry the duck, skin side down first, for about 5 minutes until brown, then turn it over and fry for another 4–5 minutes. Remove and drain.

To serve, chop the duck into small bite-size pieces (see p.68) and serve it on a bed of lettuce leaves. Or you can pull the meat off the bone and use a lettuce leaf like a puff: fill it with a few strips of duck meat, spring onions and/or shredded cucumber and a teaspoon of Hoi Sin or plum sauce; then wrap the lettuce leaf round to make a little parcel and eat with your fingers. Of course, it can also be served just like Peking duck.

o Duck soup

This simple dish is traditionally served at the end of a banquet. you will need the carcass of the duck, and its giblets if you have not already used them for another dish.

1 duck carcass (plus giblets if available)
1 lb (450 g) Chinese cabbage (or any other type of cabbage)
1–2 slices ginger root
1–2 spring onions, finely chopped
salt and pepper to taste

Break up the carcass, place it together with the giblets and any other bits and pieces in a large pot or pan, cover it with water, add the ginger root, and bring to the boil. Skim off the impurities floating on the surface, and let it simmer gently with a lid on for at least 30 minutes. Now add the washed and sliced cabbage, continue cooking for 20 minutes or so, and then it is ready.

To serve, place the finely chopped spring onions in a large bowl, pour the soup into it, adjust seasonings and serve hot.

Now, is there an easier way of making a more nourishing and delicious soup?

IX

Little Feasts and Grand Banquets

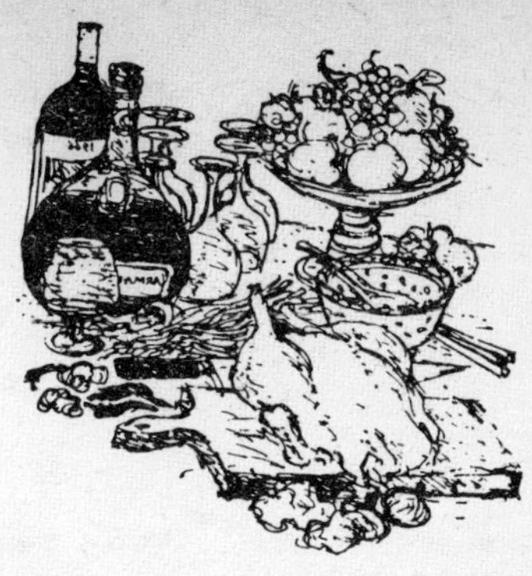

A 'little feast' in China is really only a dinner party. It need not be a special occasion: any excuse, such as the coming of spring, an appointment to a new job or just a reunion of old friends will do fine. Maybe you would simply like to show off your newly acquired skill? Should you feel slightly nervous about embarking on cooking so many new dishes all at once, why not try out a few beforehand? Trying one or two at a time a few weeks in advance will give you not only the experience you need, but also extra confidence – that is, if the dishes are successful!

With the exception of a formal occasion such as birthday or wedding celebrations, most Chinese dinner parties are of an impromptu nature. Usually the invitations are issued at short notice – sometimes only on the morning of the actual day! A special messenger will go round with the guest list and call at various addresses, and each person invited will then tick against his or her name with the word 'known'; this is normally taken to mean that the invitation has been accepted, otherwise a reason for being unable to attend would be given. One advantage of this type of invitation is that you can see at a glance who else will be there, and should you find any *persona non grata* on the list, you can always find some excuse for not being able to accept the invitation.

It is not general practice to state a precise time for the dinner on the invitation, but guests will start to arrive soon after 6 p.m.

or so, and dinner is normally served at 7 p.m., by which time all those invited should have arrived. It would be bad manners in China for any guest to turn up at a dinner party after 7 p.m. Seating arrangements also differ somewhat from the Western convention: the 'head of the table' is the seat facing the entrance and is always reserved for the guest of honour, while the host and hostess are always seated on the opposite side of the table with their backs to the door. The origin of this convention derives from an episode in the ancient history of China when a certain tyrant was stabbed in the back while being feasted by his enemies. So now the guest of honour, seated facing the door, would be the first person to see the assassin entering the room should the host have any evil intentions!

I am not suggesting that you should follow the Chinese convention of serving your dinner earlier, or that you should abandon your own traditional seating arrangements, but one Chinese custom I would like to urge you to adopt is the attitude to food. There are those of us who eat in order to live, and there are those who live in order to eat. In the case of a dinner party, the main objective should be sheer enjoyment, therefore it should take place in an informal and relaxed atmosphere. 'Don't stand on ceremony' and 'Please feel at home' should be the true mottoes of any successful party. If you must dress for dinner, then put on something that is comfortable rather than stiff and tight, so that you can really relax. It is the usual practice for a Chinese host to urge his guests to 'loosen clothing' before taking their seats at the table in order to enjoy the food and wine. Now do not get the wrong idea that the Chinese indulge themselves starkers in orgies; they merely remove their outer garments such as coats and jackets and so on, otherwise they follow rigidly a set of strict rules and conventions that have governed their table-manners and social etiquette for centuries.

Now let us get down to the more serious side of the business, namely the planning of the menu.

The order in which different courses are served at a formal Chinese meal bears no resemblance to the Western convention of soup–fish–poultry–meat–cheese–dessert sequence. For instance, soup is never served at the beginning but at the end or between courses; while sweet dishes, reserved for grand occasions, are not served at the end but in between courses or even at the beginning in the form of fruits, both fresh and dried. A whole fish is served as part of the last course because the Chinese word for fish is *yu*, which sounds exactly like the character 'to spare' in Chinese – we like to think that there is always something to spare at the very end of a meal.

On a closer examination, one soon realizes that Chinese food, like nearly everything else Chinese, is entirely governed by the *yin-yang* principle. This ancient Chinese philosophy believes that harmony arises from the proper blending of opposites, not of irreconcilable opposites but of complementary pairs.

As already mentioned, the main distinctive feature in Chinese cuisine is the emphasis on the harmonious blending of colours, aromas, flavours and textures both in one single dish and in a course of different dishes. Consciously or unconsciously, Chinese cooks, from the self-taught housewife to the professional chef, all work to the *yin-yang* principles – that is, to the harmonious balance and contrast in conspicuous juxtaposition of different colours, aromas, flavours and textures by varying the ingredients, cutting techniques, seasonings, cooking methods, and so on. Perhaps one of the best examples of the *yin-yang* principle is in the way we blend different seasonings in complementary pairs: sugar (*yin*) and vinegar (*yang*), salt (*yin*) and Sichuan pepper (*yang*), spring onion (*yin*) and ginger root (*yang*), soy sauce (*yin*) and wine (*yang*) and so on.

This principle of complementary pairs extends still further to menu planning. The order in which different courses or dishes are served depends more on the method of cooking, and the way the ingredients are prepared before cooking, than on the actual food itself. The general rules are that cold dishes are served before hot ones; quick-fried dishes before long-braised dishes; light and delicate before heavy and rich food; and on more formal occasions or at banquets, soup and/or sweet food are served in between courses to act as a neutralizer in order to cleanse the palate.

Until the beginning of this century, only square tables were used for official and formal occasions, while round tables were reserved for home and informal use. A Chinese square table can only accommodate eight persons, which used to be the standard number for feasting. How this came about perhaps can be explained by the Chinese obsession with the number 'eight', as exemplified by the *yin-yang* symbol surrounded by the Eight Trigrams, or Diagrams as they are sometimes called, which are all the possible permutations of three-line combinations of continuous (*yang*) and broken (*yin*) lines. According to Chinese belief, they form the basis of mathematics, and figuratively denote the evolution of nature, and its cyclical changes. They also served as a basis for the philosophy of divination and geomancy for the *Classic of Changes* (*I ching*, also known as the *Book of Divination*), which in turn has governed practically all aspects of Chinese way of life.

Please forgive the digression, but I have not quite finished it yet. In Taoist legends, there are eight beings who have attained immortality by having drunk the Elixir of Life – they have become known as the Eight Immortals, and their personal emblems are called the Eight Precious Things. Then the Buddhists have their Eight Symbols, and there are also Eight Lucky-emblems for us ordinary mortals; all these are sometimes called the Eight Treasures. But in cookery terms, any dish called 'eight-treasure' should consist of eight choice ingredients. In the literary world, the Tang poet Li Bai and his seven drinking companions, who were all scholars or painters besides being connoisseurs of food and wine, were given the accolade of the Eight Immortals – they were supposed to have attained immortality by excessive drinking and feasting at the table, hence a square table is also called an Eight-Immortal Table.

Nowadays in China, square tables are rarely seen outside private homes, except in some old-fashioned tea houses and inns. A standard-sized round table will seat ten people comfortably, and you can easily squeeze in an extra guest or two if necessary, so we will plan our menu for ten to twelve people.

Bear in mind that the Chinese never serve an individual dish to each person; everyone shares the dishes on the table like at a grand buffet. Remember, too, that cold and hot dishes are served separately and different courses are served one after another.

Sample Menu A

COLD STARTERS
'Agitated' prawns (p.63)
'Agitated' kidney flowers (p.59)
Sweet and sour cucumber (p.55)

TWO HOT STARTERS
Diced chicken breast with celery (p.71)
Shredded pork with green peppers (p.108)
or: Eggs with tomatoes (p.98)
Fried fish slices (p.152)

MAIN COURSES (SERVED WITH RICE)
West Lake beef soup (p.51)
Red-cooked pork shoulder (p.131)
Steamed whole fish (p.155)
Fried spinach *or* lettuce (p.92)

DESSERT
Fruit (p.4)

Sample Menu B

COLD STARTER
Sliced chicken with ham and broccoli (p.82)

TWO HOT STARTERS
Fried prawns with mange-touts peas (p.158)
Stir-fried kidney flowers (p.134)
or: Chicken slices and bamboo shoots (p.77)
Scallops with mixed vegetables (p.162)

MAIN COURSES (SERVED WITH RICE)
Braised duck (p.174)
Braised brisket of beef (p.128)
Sweet and sour fish (p.164)
Fish head soup (p.165)

DESSERT
Fruit salad (p.4)

Sample Menu C

STARTERS
Crystal-boiled pork (p.58)
Pickled radishes (p.56)
Phoenix-tail prawns (p.62)

PRINCIPAL DISH
Roast duck Peking style (p.170)
or: Aromatic and crispy duck (p.176)

MAIN COURSES (SERVED WITH RICE)
Braised fish steak (p.150)
Fu-yung (Lotus-white) chicken (p.83)
Beef in oyster sauce (p.130)
Pork and french beans (p.105)
or: Fish slices and mushrooms assembly (p.163)
Braised chicken with green peppers (p.69)
Fricassée spare ribs (p.123)
Braised Chinese cabbage (p.90)

SOUP
Duck soup (p.177)

Since first course dishes are served cold, they can all be prepared beforehand. Most of the main course dishes can also be prepared and cooked in advance, but all the stir-fried dishes require last-minute cooking. So a precise schedule is essential, otherwise your dinner party may turn into a fiasco!

Unless you and your guests are teetotallers, you cannot possibly do without wine for a feast; in fact it will not be a feast at all even though you have taken a lot of trouble in the kitchen.

As you will have gathered from the sample menus (pp.185–6), a formal Chinese dinner usually starts with light and delicate dishes, then gradually progresses to heavier and richer dishes. With this as a guide, you can now choose your wine for each course without much difficulty. To start with, as an aperitif as well as to go with the cold hors d'oeuvres, serve any light white wine such as Muscadet, Graves, Sauvignon or Chardonnay. For those who prefer a less dry white wine, serve hock or Moselle, or a Riesling – in fact the choice is almost limitless: there is always a wide range of sound and delicate white wines at your disposal. Of course you need not confine yourself to whites only; for those who like it, a rosé, and indeed a sparkling wine or champagne, will also be fine.

For the next course, when you are eating the fried dishes, a big, full-bodied wine with plenty of fruit and flavour such as Alsace, Côtes du Rhône, Pouilly Blanc Fumé, Chablis or Rioja should be served; or, for those who prefer red wine, Beaujolais, Chinon, Bourgueil or any other light and fruity red wine – again the choice is wide.

A more robust wine is called for to serve with the main course. There is no need for you to follow the Chinese convention of not serving wine with 'rice dishes', bearing in mind that the Italians always drink wine with their risotto and the Spaniards with their paella, not to mention the French with their various rice dishes. What you need is a full-bodied and strongly flavoured red to offset the rather rich quality of the food. So for the claret lovers, I would suggest the aromatic, generous yet soft Pomerol or St Emilion, although personally I would prefer a firmer and fruitier minor burgundy such as Beaune or Volnay. Also a powerful and fragrant Châteauneuf-du-Pape or Hermitage will be a success. Equally the Italian Rubesco, Barolo and Barbaresco or the Spanish Rioja are all fruity and fragrant as well as robust wines, but like all great wine they require many years to mature. Further afield, there are good Cabernet Sauvigons from California, Australia and South America and so on.

When does a feast become a banquet? According to my dictionary, a feast is a sumptuous meal while a banquet is a sumptuous feast. So there you are!

After the success, or should I say the triumph, of your little feast, what better way to celebrate it than to have a banquet as a follow-up?

The main point to remember in planning your banquet is that you cannot expect top quality food when cooking in large quantities, so if you are having twenty-four guests instead of twelve, do not double the amount of ingredients used, but rather increase the number of dishes and courses so that not only will you achieve a better result, but also there will be a larger variety of food for your guests to marvel at and enjoy. Nor is it necessary to stick to the 'one dish per person' rule. For instance, fourteen to sixteen dishes should be more than enough for twenty or more people. Personally, I think no feast or banquet should exceed sixteen dishes, however sumptuous you want it to be; otherwise it would be too much of an expense, both in time and money.

So a sample menu will run very much on the same lines as the little feast:

First course: Four or five cold starters served simultaneously in individual dishes, or neatly arranged into a pattern on a large plate and served as an assorted hors d'oeuvre. The dishes are chosen for their harmonious contrast and balance in colour, flavour and texture, but they should include the three basic 'meats' (i.e. fish, chicken and meat) plus a vegetable. If it is at all practical, select eight (that magical Number 8 again!) different items for the assorted hors d'oeuvre. Because of the large number of different ingredients used, you need only a small quantity of each item for this dish, but remember not to have more than one of the same type of food. For instance, if you use braised duck, then do not serve soy-braised chicken at the same time, but use cold sliced chicken instead; similarly, do not serve phoenix-tail prawns and prawns in shells at the same banquet. The following is a suggested list:

1. 'Smoked' fish (p.61)
2. 'Agitated' prawns (p.63)
3. Cold sliced chicken (p.26)
4. Fragrant pork (p.57)
5. Duck liver in wine sauce (p.172)
6. Braised duck (p.174)
7. Braised tripe (p.60)
8. Braised eggs (p.56)
9. Sweet and sour cucumber (p.55)
10. Pickled radishes (p.56)

Second course: Four or five hot starters to be served one or two at a time; these are usually stir-fried, deep-fried or quick-braised dishes such as prawns in shells, sesame seed prawn toast, stir-fried prawns and peas, diced chicken with green peppers, chicken slices and bamboo shoots, stir-fried kidney flowers, fried beef and tomatoes, meat slices with spring onions, pork laurel (mu-shu pork), stir-fried liver with Wooden Ears, duck giblets assembly, etc – the range is almost limitless, and one can go on almost indefinitely. Again, bear in mind the *yin-yang* principle of complementary pairs and do not serve the same type of food either together or in the same course.

Third course: In China, at this stage of a formal banquet, it is customary to serve what is known as the 'principal dish', a thickish 'soup' which gives the banquet its title. For instance, if a shark's fin soup is served, then it is called a *shark's fin banquet*; and if a birds' nest soup is served, then it is called a *birds' nest banquet*. These two top-ranking delicacies used to be a must at all grand banquets, but nowadays it is quite acceptable to serve sea cucumber, also known as *bêche-de-mer*, or sea slug. Further down the scale is abalone, and at the bottom of the ladder is fish maw, the bladder of the yellow croaker, a sea fish. I have not included any of these 'five delicacies from the sea' of Chinese cuisine in the preceding sections for good reasons. To start with, they are all very expensive and tedious to prepare before they become edible, particularly the two most highly regarded items, therefore they cannot be regarded as everyday home food; then they are quite flavourless with a rather strange texture – I have yet to meet a Westerner who can truly appreciate any of them apart from their exotic appeal. In China, too many people are cajoled into liking them purely because of their rarity value; what they may not realize is that unless they are cooked with chicken, ham, etc, all the so-called 'delicacies' are quite tasteless. Here I would like to quote you one of China's foremost scholar-gourmets, Yuan Mei (1716–1798) who wrote in the *Sui Yuan Cookery Book*:

> I always say that chicken, pork, fish and duck are the original geniuses of the board, each with a flavour of its own, each with its distinctive character; whereas *bêche-de-mer* and birds' nest, despite their costliness, are common-place fellows, without character – in fact, mere hangers-on. I was once asked to a dinner party given by a certain Governor, who gave us plain boiled birds' nest, served in enormous vases like flower-pots. It was quite tasteless, but all the other guests were obsequious in their praise of it. Our host's object was simply to impress. I thought it would have been better if a hundred pearls were put into each bowl, then we should have known that the meal had cost him dearly, without the unpleasantness of being expected to eat what was uneatable.

So, as a compromise, I suggest that you serve *san-xian* (three-delicacies) soup to act as a breather before the main course's 'big' dishes. Remember, only a very small portion is required for each guest.

Main course: Four 'big' dishes, which should be a whole chicken, duck, fish, and pork leg or shoulder. Since this is the main course of the banquet, the conversation will become subdued and serious eating commence, for until now all the other dishes have only been a warming-up to get you into the right mood for the final assault. Towards the end of the main course, a large bowl of steaming hot soup is served. The soup is usually made out of the bones from the main course with vegetables added. But very often a light, clear soup or even a sweet dish would be served (see below).

Dessert: Served only at formal banquets, usually between courses. At less grand occasions soup is often served at the end of the meal.

Final course: Paradoxically, steamed dumplings, fried rice or/and fried noodles, which are regarded as snacks (*dim sum*) and are never served at everyday meals, will make their appearance at the very end of a grand banquet so that nobody can complain of still feeling hungry afterwards!

Fresh fruit and hot tea will make a most welcome appearance right at the end of the meal.

My dear readers, I do hope you have enjoyed reading and trying out some of the recipes in this book. I am sure you will agree that there is really no mystery involved in Chinese cooking once you have learnt the basic principles: that the most important points to remember when selecting ingredients are colour, aroma, flavour and texture; that the success of a particular dish depends on the blending and harmonizing of these elements; and that, to a large extent, the same applies to planning a menu, where the accent is on harmony and contrast in order to achieve a good balance.

I cannot emphasize enough the importance of fully preparing all the ingredients before the actual cooking, for if you have all the materials well prepared and set out within easy reach you should feel relaxed and will avoid last-minute panic. There is not much point in cooking if you do not enjoy it, so you must preserve peace of mind in order to cook a good meal.

The late Harold Wilshaw once said when he was the cookery writer for the *Guardian*: 'Quite my favourite way of spending any money which comes my way is to have friends round my table, eating my food and drinking my wine. I have no car or television set, and so the money I do not spend on those two boring adjuncts to modern living, I spend giving little luncheons and dinners.' I think he had definitely got the right approach to life, and only wish more people would adopt the same attitude, thus creating a happier and healthier world for all of us.

X

What to Drink with Chinese Food

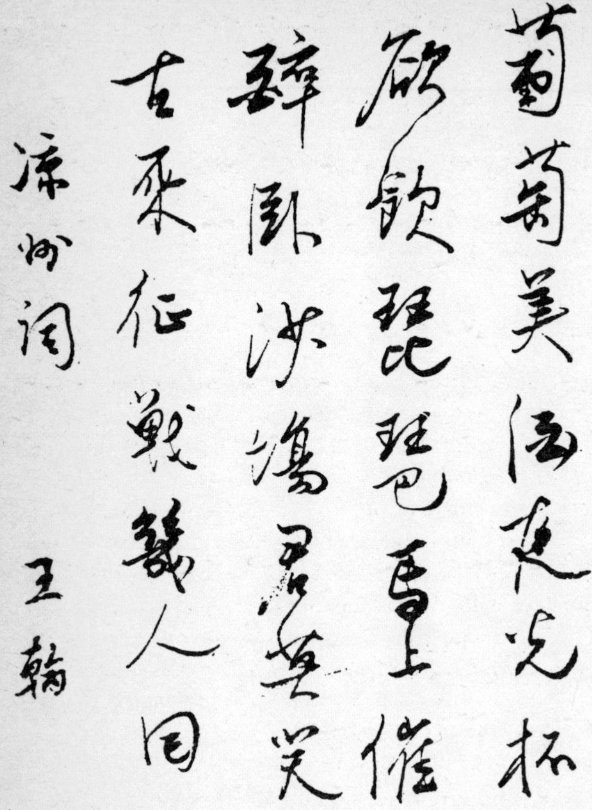

Beautiful grape wine glittering a white jade goblet:
I was just about to drink it when the lute was sounded, hastening me to mount my horse.
Should I lie drunk on the battlefield beyond the Great Wall, please don't laugh at me,
For how many warriors have returned home from an expedition since the ancient days?

Wang Han: Song of the Western Region

Perhaps it was this eighth-century poem, taught to me by my grandfather when I was about seven, that first awakened my interest in wine. In contrast to their sophisticated approach to food and the high development of their culinary art, the Chinese as a whole are remarkably indifferent to alcoholic drinks. With the exception of the connoisseur, the Chinese do not normally distinguish between wine from the fermented juice of fruits and grains, and spirit in which the alcohol content is much higher as a result of distillation. In everyday usage, the word *jiu* or *chiew* means any type of alcoholic beverage – in the same way as 'wine' is used generally in the West when we refer to the 'wine list' in a restaurant or a 'wine merchant' and so on.

But it is interesting to note here that in ancient China (Shang dynasty beginning around 1500 BC), different types of bronze and pottery drinking utensils were used for different alcoholic beverages, and Zhou (beginning around 1028 BC) texts use different words to distinguish different kinds of wines. Textual accounts and archaeological finds point to the indulgence of Shang noblemen in their drinking habits. We also know that alcoholic beverages were an indispensable part of feasts, meals and important ritual occasions of both Shang and Zhou periods; they were also used as a seasoning in cooking.

We have in Chinese (both ancient and modern) a word for food and drink combined: *yinshi*, a compound word made up of *yin* (to drink) and *shi* (to eat). Now since the Chinese do not drink water with their meals, nor tea either, except for a small minority of people in certain parts of China (at any rate, tea did not become an everyday drink until the second half of the eighth century), we must assume that the Chinese have integrated alcoholic beverages with their eating habits. In cookery terms we make the clear distinction between 'wine dishes' (*juicai*) and 'rice dishes' (*fancai*). Usually the 'wine dishes' consist of cold *hors d'oeuvres* and hot starters (mostly quick stir-fried, deep-fried or quick-braised dishes) which are meant to accompany wine drinking before rice is served with the main course. Only when drinking is finished do the Chinese start to eat rice with the 'rice dishes'. I was told that because almost all Chinese wines (I am using the word 'wine' here to cover any kind of alcoholic beverage, in the true Chinese manner!) are made from grains such as rice and millet, it is considered sacrilegious to drink alcohol with rice. This is a deep-rooted belief. At less formal occasions or at ordinary meals when all the dishes are served together, the Chinese would take a drink, eat something that is on the table, then drink again, thus imbibing between mouthfuls of food before beginning their bowl of rice. Those who enjoy a drink before eating are westernized Chinese, myself being one of them, having lived for more than thirty years in the West.

All that was just to dispel the misconception commonly held in the West that Chinese food and wine do not go well together. Some people regard Chinese food as too 'spicy' for wine, but how about the French *bouquet garni*? – not to mention the onions, garlic and tomatoes etc widely used in all the Mediterranean cooking. Then there are those who recommend a white wine for *all* Chinese food; obviously that cannot be right either unless you happen to dislike drinking red wine.

Readers will notice that my own preference is for French wines. This is entirely personal, for wine drinking is a very personal thing, and it does not mean that I dislike wines that are not French. On the contrary, I am perfectly aware that a great many excellent wines are made all over the world, but it would be quite impossible to recommend them all here. Suffice it to say that when I mention a certain name such Beaujolais, then Italian wines of a similar nature, such as Bardolino or Valpolicella, will do just as well, or indeed any light and refreshing wine – Californian, Australian or Spanish wines are equally suitable.

Since each course of a Chinese meal usually consists of a number of different dishes, it is almost impossible to match a particular wine with a particular dish. But I would stick my neck out and declare that *all* red burgundies are excellent accompaniments for *all* Chinese food, seafood included. Having said that, I must qualify my statement somewhat by further declaring that certain dishes (not necessarily seafood) will go particularly well with a white wine.

Take the famous dish, Peking duck, for example. I always used to drink a red wine with it, and thought it was an excellent partnership until a friend served a white burgundy (it was a Puligny-Montrachet) at his dinner. The effect was sensational! Never before had I experienced such a wonderful flavour which lingered on in the mouth with a combination of such richness and subtlety. A true Franco–Chinese *entente*, you might call it.

I have already pointed out that in China it is not the natural taste of the food but rather the method of cooking that determines the order of its appearance at the table, so that you start off with light dishes and then go on to heavier and richer ones. This makes it convenient to serve a lighter wine first, be it white or red, then go on to a more robust and full-bodied wine with a richer flavour. For instance, at a dinner some years back I served a young Pouilly-Vinzelles with cold sliced chicken and deep-fried prawns; this was followed by a three-year-old Morgon, to go with sesame seed prawn toast, beef in oyster sauce, diced chicken breast and stir-fried kidney flowers. I also opened a 1966 Chambolle-Musigny which had a great delicacy and finesse with a superb bouquet, whereas the Morgon was lighter with a delightful fruitiness. After the soup came the 'big' dishes: fragrant pork and red-cooked fish. We drank a 1959 Clos de

Vougeot which was soft, supple and elegant with an aromatic bouquet. Some people may be horrified at the idea of drinking a Clos de Vougeot with fish, but this particular dish had such a rich sauce that no ordinary white wine would have been robust enough to partner it perfectly.

On another occasion we started with a Riesling from Alsace for the cold hors d'oeuvres; then for the next course, which consisted of stir-fried hot dishes (both fish and meat), we had a four-year-old Julienas which had a brilliant purple colour coupled with a very fruity nose and was rich in taste with the quality of 'plumpness' which normally could only be found in a great burgundy. This turned out to be a perfect prelude to our next wine, a 1964 Bonnes Mares; though over ten years old, it had a deep ruby colour, flowery bouquet and an exceptional finesse, combining body with strength. We all agreed that it was such a lively wine that it still had a long way to go before its peak.

Maurice Healy was once quoted as saying that one will only drink four or five bottles of truly first-class burgundy in one's life – and be lucky at that. In that respect I must count myself as really lucky, for so far I have already had more than my fair share in my short life and, at the risk of being accused of greed, I am looking forward to many more great bottles still to come.

The most memorable bottle I ever had was in 1974 at the hospitable table of Mr and Mrs S. K. Ho, two family friends, who opened a 1959 Richebourg, Domaine de la Romanée-Conti, to go with a roast duck with stuffings and several other wonderful dishes. I have no doubt about the excellence and deliciousness of the food, as the late Mrs Ho was a first-class cook, but to be honest, all I can remember today is the Richebourg. What a velvety softness, combined with a rich fragrance that lingered on long afterwards. Its distinctive flavour was fascinating and impossible to describe. 'Magnificent' was the one word that immediately came to mind.

Since these words were written just over a decade ago, the price of burgundy has rocketed so high that it is far beyond the reach of most of us, therefore I would recommend a good

Beaujolais as the ideal red wine for all Chinese food. I use the word 'good' here to emphasize the importance of careful choice when selecting a Beaujolais. It is said that such is the demand for this wine that more 'Beaujolais' is drunk in Paris in a year than is produced in the whole district. I find that because of the enormous quantity of Beaujolais produced each year, the quality varies a great deal. Therefore even a genuine Beaujolais can be rather indifferent in some cases. I think it is worth paying a little extra to buy bottles that bear a *commune* name (and a single vineyard can be even better). My favourites are Julienas, Fleurie, Morgon, and Côtes de Brouilly, in that order.

What is it that make Beaujolais so attractive to most people? I think the answer must be its light yet firm body, its fragrant and fruity nose, and above all its distinctive flavour which, though difficult to describe, is immediately recognizable. Once you have tasted the genuine article an ordinary 'Beaujolais' will taste either too heavy or too watery, but in either case without much fruit and without a very distinctive flavour.

A good red Mâcon also represents good value for money, as it is generally cheaper than a Beaujolais but not necessarily inferior. The famous Pouilly Fuissé, a refreshing dry white wine, comes from this district. I find it has a more delicious nose and more depth of flavour than the more expensive Chablis from farther to the north.

With claret, the English name for red Bordeaux, things are much brighter. To start with more than six times as much wine is produced each year in Bordeaux than in Burgundy, therefore good claret of high quality is easily available in abundance, sometimes even at a fairly reasonable price.

What is the difference in taste between a claret and a burgundy? The answer is, very little. They are the two greatest red wines in the world, and the differences are very subtle and therefore difficult to define. Some people will tell you that claret is a light, delicate and dry wine, while burgundy is heavy, rich and sweet. This generalization makes it sound as though they were two entirely different wines. Far from it: if you compare a claret and a burgundy of the same quality you will find there are more similarities between them than, say, between a so-called Spanish 'burgundy' and the genuine thing.

No true wine-lover could honestly declare that one is a better wine than the other; it is purely a matter of personal preference. At a blind tasting it is extremely hard even for the experts to distinguish the two wines. Cyril Ray, in his highly entertaining *In a Glass Lightly* (Methuen), unfortunately now out of print, recounts the story of how Harry Waugh, a legendary character in the wine trade for his skill and judgement as a taster, was once asked whether he had ever mistaken a burgundy for a claret and gave the rueful reply: 'Not since luncheon.'

One of the commonest mistakes some people make when they complain that claret tastes sour and harsh is that they drink the wine long before it is ready. Unlike a burgundy, which takes on average five to six years to mature and will become drinkable within three or four years of the vintage, a claret will take much longer to reach its peak and while it is being matured is never quite so drinkable as a burgundy of the same age. It will not have much nose or flavour, and it will taste sour and hard because it has no balance of acidity and tannin which protects the young wine and helps its development to maturity. A high-quality claret of a good vintage will take at least ten years to mature; it will then have a powerful and distinctive bouquet, a fine, fruity flavour with real depth. It will be a *great* wine of an overwhelming beauty that tends to linger in your glass even when it has been drained to the last drop.

Rhône wines are very popular, partly because they represent good value for money. But you have to choose your plain Côtes du Rhône very carefully as the wines vary quite a bit. I think wines that are bottled by the growers themselves are usually safest. Otherwise pay a little extra for a *commune* wine such as Hermitage or Côte Rôtie; both are robust and full of character with the latter slightly softer and lighter. These and Châteauneuf-du-Pape, the biggest of them all, should really be left to mature for at least five to eight years in bottle; then they become richer and fuller with real flavour and scent, like lovely ripe fruit; they will go beautifully with most Chinese food.

While we are in the south of France, do not overlook the cheaper *vins de pays*, particularly the VDQS (*Vins délimités de qualité supérieure*) such as Costières du Gard, Corbières, Côtes du Roussillon and Coteaux d'Aix-en-Provence to name just a few. Then there are those higher-graded *appellation contrôlée* wines of Côtes de Provence. I should also single out the red wines from Bandol, not far from Marseilles. Whenever I am in the Midi, I always make a point of stopping there in order to taste and select a few bottles to bring back to London. I find them excellent with a number of Chinese dishes.

Readers will have gathered that I am a Francophile as far as taste in wine is concerned. I hasten to add that I do drink, and have enjoyed, wine from other countries, only I do not feel I know enough about any of them to do justice to them. Perhaps I should just mention that I find the Spanish Rioja wonderful value as well as highly enjoyable. As for some of the fine Italian wines, besides the famous Chianti Classico, names I remember are Barolo, Bardolino and Rubesco di Torgiano for red, Frascati and Soave for white.

I have also enjoyed wines from the Napa Valley in California. Undoubtedly the best one is a white called Chardonnay, named after the burgundy grape from which it is made. It is crisp and dry, full of scent and fruit – a truly great wine. The best red I have tasted is Cabernet Sauvignon (the principal red grape of Bordeaux); it is not unlike a good claret, with plenty of body and flavour. In comparison, the Pinot Noir (the noble red grape of Burgundy) is less successful, though it is still a good wine. Here again, I feel I have not sampled enough varieties to make any fair comment on a great wine district.

Australia has also produced some great wines. The two grapes that once dominated their wine-making – Shiraz or Hermitage for red, and the Semillon or Riesling for white, are being edged aside by the Cabernet Sauvignon and Chardonnay. This is partly due to the French firm Remy Martin, famous not only for their cognacs but also controlling the Krug champagne house as well as the Bordeaux negoçiants de Luze. Much replanting and new technology have revolutionized Australia's wine industry, to the advantage of us all.

Following the Australian example, China has now also enlisted the help of the French oenologists (from the same Remy Martin group) to develop their very modest wine industry. As a result, the Sino-French Joint Venture Winery Ltd was set up in the late 1970s just outside Tianjin, China's third largest city lying not very far southeast of Peking. They initially planted 37,500 acres (15,000 hectares) of vines from the native stock. Their first vintage, a white wine under the brand name Dynasty was unveiled at the Vinexpo wine trade fair in Bordeaux in the summer of 1981. I was present at a special London tasting organized by Dynasty's UK distributor later that year, and I tasted the wine again on a number of subsequent occasions. I found it to be medium dry, not without fruit, but not all that well balanced. Since then, efforts have been made to plant vine of noble *Vitis vinifera* extraction to improve the quality.

While the development of a wine industry is obviously a long-term project, it appears that China has entered a new era in quality wine-making: it was reported in 1985 that premium wines produced in Qingdao (Tsingtao), Shandong Peninsular were expected to be about 150 cases of Chardonnay and approximately 10,000 cases of Riesling. Experiments were being made with Cabernet to produce various styles of wine. I would only be deluding myself if I thought that Chinese wines could be compared with any of the top-quality products from the Mediterranean and its neighbouring countries. Nevertheless, since China lies within the temperate zones, surely there must be an area which contains the right soil for the right grape, and once she has found the right spot and acquired the know-how, given time there is no reason why China should not be able to produce wines on a par with, say, California, Argentina or Australia.

As you might well imagine, in a country where rice is the staple food, rice wine is the most popular beverage in China.

There must be literally hundreds of different varieties of rice wine in China, but very little is exported. *Shaoxing Chiew*, which is widely available in the West, is the pearl of all Chinese rice wine, mainly because of the water used for its brewing. Shaoxing is situated south of Hangzhou in Zhejiang province, and its wine-making history dates back to 470 BC for it was recorded in the District Chronicle. The main ingredients are glutinous rice, millet and ordinary rice. The water comes from a large lake which draws its source from the fountains and streams that flow down the sandy rock mountains on one side and the dense bamboo-forested hills on the other. The water is so clear and the surface so smooth that the lake is also known as 'The Mirror', and it has a high mineral content.

There are several varieties of Shaoxing wine. The most famous and popular is *Hua Diao* ('Carved Flower'), so-called because of the pretty patterns carved on the urns in which the wines are stored for maturing in underground cellars. The best ones are supposed to be over a hundred years old, but those offered for sale on the market nowadays are probably about ten years old and should be deep amber in colour. Once I tasted one that was over forty years old; when the seal of the urn was broken the bouquet was so tremendously powerful that it filled the entire room (which was quite large) and lingered in the air for hours.

Another name for *Hua Diao* is 'Daughter's Wine' because it used to be the local custom to store a few urns of Shaoxing wine at the birth of a daughter to be given as part of her dowry and to be consumed at her wedding feast (normally seventeen to nineteen years later). It is interesting to compare this charming tradition with the male-oriented British custom of laying down port for a son for his twenty-first birthday.

Another Chinese tradition which is not confined just to Shaoxing district is the custom at weddings when the bride and groom each drinks half a cup of wine then exchange the cups and finish the other half. Sometimes couples will share the same cup, each drinking half, a sign that they are now man and wife and that they will love and respect one another for ever.

When you drink wine, sheer pleasure should be your prime motivation. That it increases the enjoyment of food, facilitates your digestion and thereby improves your health, and so on, is undoubtedly true, but I rather suspect people who try to justify their reasons for drinking wine – they must secretly have a guilt complex. Like sex, wine is one of the pleasures of life that you do not need to have an excuse for. 'Wine, women and song!' Give me them any day!

But like all good things in life, excessive and indiscrimate application is to be positively avoided. Therefore a few basic points in regard to selecting and serving wine should be observed in order to enchance its enjoyment. One need not be too dogmatic about the 'rules', such as they are, but should use one's own common sense and imagination. Trial and error is a much better way of gaining experience.

Having one way or another bought your wine, be it of high quality or *vin ordinaire*, treat it with respect. Unless it is to be consumed within a short time, say two or three weeks, the bottle or bottles should be stored, horizontally, in a dark, cool place. Avoid any vibration or sudden change of temperature. That is why an underground cellar is an ideal place for storage of wine. But how many of us have cellar space nowadays? Nevertheless, an even temperature is more important than coolness; only bear in mind that wines stored in a warm place will mature more quickly.

All white wine, sherry and champagne included, should be served slightly chilled. If it is served too cold, much of the bouquet and flavour will be lost. Most red wine should be served at room temperature. This is best achieved by standing the bottle in the dining room for twenty-four hours or more (hence the term *chambré*). Under no circumstances should the bottle be immersed in hot water or placed in front of a fire. Such acts are detrimental to any wine – except Chinese rice wine or Japanese *sake*, which should always be served lukewarm, ideally at body temperature.

My grandmother used to make a quite sweet but potent glutinous rice wine, and I was first introduced to it at an early age: I got quite drunk when I was only four.

It happened like this: my grandmother let me taste a small cupful of her new home-brew. I liked it so much that when her back was turned I just helped myself from the big urn. To this day I can still recall the aroma that greeted me when I lifted the lid of the wine urn, having climbed up on a footstool – for the urn was as tall as me – and as I peeped down the narrow opening I could see my little face reflected on the surface of the beautiful liquor. What happened after that has become rather blurred. I believe they found me sound asleep at the foot of the wine urn, and drew the obvious conclusions!

This was long before I had read *Yinshi Chengyao* ('The Correct Guide To Drinks and Food') by the Imperial Physician of the Yuan Dynasty, first published in 1330. In the chapter on wine, the following points are to be noted:

Do not over-indulge yourself when drinking wine.

If you must get drunk, do not be dead drunk otherwise you will feel ill for the rest of your life.

Do not drink wine continuously: it is bad for your stomach.

When drunk, do not ride a horse or jump about: you may injure yourself.

When drunk, do not have sexual intercourse, it will give you a spotty face in a mild case, or worse still, diarrhoea and piles.

When drunk, do not lose your temper or shout loudly.

When drunk, do not fall asleep in draughts.

Never drink wine without food.

Avoid sweet food with wine.

Do not lift heavy weights if drunk.

Do not take a bath if drunk, it will give you an eye ailment.

If you have an eye infection, avoid getting drunk and eating garlic at the same time. [Well!]

There is certainly quite a lot of sound advice here, but I fail to see any logic in some of it! Anyway, you have now been warned.

APPENDIX

The Art of Tea Drinking

It is a curious fact that tea and wine drinking do not seem to go together. Yet the enjoyment of both lies in appreciation of the three basic essentials: colour, fragrance and flavour. Li Yu, the seventeenth-century Chinese epicure-poet, stated quite categorically in his book on the art of living that great drinkers of tea are not fond of wine, and vice versa. Being a wine lover myself, I therefore feel unqualified to talk about the art of tea drinking as we know it in China.

In my family, my grandmother had a great capacity for wine but treated tea merely as a thirst-quenching beverage; while my grandfather, a teetotaller, was a true tea connoisseur. I used to accompany him to the tea shops to select his favourite tea – in China, we have shops that sell nothing but tea, rather like the old-fashioned wine merchants in England where a customer is usually treated with respect and courtesy.

A Chinese tea connoisseur attaches great importance to the preparation in tea making, particularly the type of water used. It is generally agreed that mountain spring water is best, river water second and well water third. Water from the tap, being contaminated with metal and treated with chemicals, is most unsatisfactory. Similarly, never use a brass kettle or one of any other metal, the ideal one is made of earthenware. Avoid using damp firewood on account of the smoke, always use freshly boiled water, and so on. And most important of all, the tea itself. I think it is true to say that there are almost as many varieties of tea in China as there are wines in France.

Most tea-producing countries grow only one, or at most a few varieties – black tea in India, Sri Lanka and Kenya, and green teas in Japan. China, on the other hand, produces a very wide range which can be divided into five main categories: black, green, scented, oolong and brick.

Black teas are processed by fermenting. They have a fresh, strong flavour and often a honey-like aroma. The Chinese call them 'red' teas because of the colour of the brewed tea, rather than 'black' which is the colour of the tea leaves. The most famous black tea is Keemun Black, produced in southeast China.

Green teas are dried and roasted (like the black) but not fermented. They are consequently lighter and more subtly flavoured. The best known is Long Jing (Dragon Well) and is produced in Hangzhou.

Oolong tea, which is semi-fermented, is a special product of Fujian province, and the most famous variety is Tie Guanyin (The Iron Goddess). Oolong teas are particularly popular in parts of south China and among expatriate Chinese in South-East Asia.

Scented teas are prepared by adding dried flower petals such as jasmine, magnolia and rose to high quality green tea.

Brick teas are essentially black teas, fermented, roasted and dried, then compressed into oblong 'bricks'. They can be stored for a long time without losing their flavour.

Some people find tea an ideal substitute for an *apéritif* before a meal – particularly in the middle of the day when they may want to cut down their alcoholic intake. It certainly helps to clean your palate, and after a good Chinese meal nothing is more refreshing than a large pot of hot tea – clear, pale or scented and *without* milk and sugar.

Index

All recipes are shown in italics